P9-BZT-388

Mt. Lebanon Public Library
16 Castle Shannon Blvd.
Pittsburgh, PA 15228-2252
412-531-1912
www.mtlebanonlibrary.org
Children's Library   10/2017

DISCARDED
MT LEBANON...

ADVANCE PRAISE FOR
THE NOTATIONS OF COOPER CAMERON:

"Cooper Cameron is a unique and unforgettable character, a boy who sees the beauty in bugs and the heroism in frogs."
—Kurtis Scaletta, author of *Mudville* and
Rooting for Rafael Rosales

PRAISE FOR JANE O'REILLY'S
THE SECRET OF GOLDENROD:

A Junior Library Guild Selection

Kirkus Reviews' Best Middle-Grade Books of 2016

★ "[S]hines with wisdom and compassion."
—starred, *Kirkus Reviews*

★ "[A] wistful and superlative coming-of-age story . . . this is one to be re-read and enjoyed many times over."
—starred, *Booklist*

"[A] unique twist on the traditional haunted house story."
—*School Library Journal*

"A bewitching and beautiful story of haunted houses, family secrets, and life-changing friends found in the most unexpected of places. Like the mysterious mansion at the heart of the book, Jane O'Reilly's writing is magical."
—Anne Ursu, author of *Breadcrumbs* and *The Real Boy*

"*The Secret of Goldenrod* is replete with elements of a children's classic: yearning, solitude, hope, friendship, and most of all, magic. An utterly dear book."
—Jane St. Anthony, author of
Isabelle Day Refuses to Die of a Broken Heart

the NOTATIONS of COOPER CAMERON

JANE O'REILLY

CAROLRHODA BOOKS
MINNEAPOLIS

Text copyright © 2017 by Jane O'Reilly

All rights reserved. International copyright secured. No part of this book may be reproduced, stored in a retrieval system, or transmitted in any form or by any means—electronic, mechanical, photocopying, recording, or otherwise—without the prior written permission of Lerner Publishing Group, Inc., except for the inclusion of brief quotations in an acknowledged review.

Carolrhoda Books
A division of Lerner Publishing Group, Inc.
241 First Avenue North
Minneapolis, MN 55401 USA

For reading levels and more information, look up this title at www.lernerbooks.com.

Illustrations by Julie McLaughlin

Main body text set in Bembo Std regular 12.5/17.
Typeface provided by Monotype Typography.

Library of Congress Cataloging-in-Publication Data

The Cataloging-in-Publication Data for *The Notations of Cooper Cameron* at the Library of Congress.
ISBN 978-1-5124-0415-9 (trade hardcover)
ISBN 978-1-5124-4853-5 (eb pdf)

LC record available at https://lccn.loc.gov/2016042763

Manufactured in the United States of America
1-39198-21095-3/29/2017

FOR CATHERINE

JUNE BUGS

"Cooper, the pizza will be here any minute," his mother calls from the kitchen. "Caddie, please help me set the table."

Cooper runs to the dining room window. Pepperoni pizza is his favorite. He watches the street for the pizza car with the Piping Hot Pizza hat on its roof. The car will look like a taxi.

A girl flutters by on her bike. The reflectors blink like fireflies in the shadows. And then a June bug hits the window screen with a sudden bang and a frantic buzzing of wings. Cooper blinks, startled. He reaches into his pocket and pulls out his pocket-size notebook and stubby pencil and makes a note to himself.

The coleopteran is a beetle and should be called a May bug because it is still May, not June.

1

"What do you want to drink, Coop?" Caddie says.

Cooper flicks the window screen with his finger. The beetle curls its legs, hangs on for dear life. Now Cooper thinks about catching bugs with Grandpa. Jars and jars of coleoptera, cicadas, and his favorite, the Lampyridae. Fireflies. Magical, blinking fireflies. He can still hear Grandpa's voice. "There you go, my boy. A flashlight in a jar." He sees the look on Grandpa's face, gray and afraid. Sees his hand drop the oar, grip the side of the boat. He wonders if Grandpa hung on for dear life.

Don't think about Grandpa. Don't think about Grandpa. Don't think about Grandpa.

Think about summer vacation. No teachers watching him. No classmates copying him behind his back. No one saying, "That boy is so weird."

He has passed fifth grade with flying colors. "Cooper can read at the college level," the counselor told his mother. "Can read anything you put in front of him." And he does. He even reads the encyclopedia. And things he's not supposed to read, like Caddie's magazines and her girl books. He reads more than anyone else he knows because he reads every word three times, every line three times, and every page three times.

But he reads fast so no one notices. And he hides this secret because no one will understand. If they find out, they might have to send him away.

Away. Away. Away.

When school starts again in the fall he will be in sixth grade. "Yeah, right," his father said. "If they let him back in the classroom."

"Cooper!" Caddie says with mad in her voice.

"Water," he says.

The June bug shivers against the screen and flies away. Cooper turns the page in his notebook.

Soon all the coleoptera will disappear without notice.

Like getting over the hiccups.

Except Cooper notices everything. He hears the plates clink as his mother lifts them from the kitchen cupboard. Behind him, Caddie folds paper napkins and sets them at the edge of the placemats. His father has flipped open his wallet so he can pay the Piping Hot Pizza delivery man. "All I have are ones," his father says with a lot of mad in his voice.

Here it comes. The beat-up car with the Piping Hot Pizza hat. Headlights bounce in the driveway.

"The Piping Hot Pizza is here," Cooper says in a happy voice, just like he's supposed to. Just like a regular kid.

The doorbell rings.

Cooper beats Caddie to the dining room table. To the tilting stack of dollar bills. "Don't, Cooper. Dad'll get mad," Caddie whispers.

Dad will get mad. Dad will get mad. Dad will get mad.

He always gets mad. "There's something wrong with That Boy," booms in Cooper's head. "That Boy needs help," booms and booms and booms.

There is something wrong with The Father too. The Father is always angry. But Cooper would never say such a thing out loud.

Still, Cooper can't help himself. The dollar bills are a mess. No one cares about them. "One, two, three," he begins to count them. Turns them right side up.

Cooper isn't doing anything wrong. It's That Boy. That Boy won't leave him alone.

But sometimes Cooper is glad That Boy is there. Sometimes he needs That Boy. That Boy worries about the girl on the bike. In the dark. Worries about all the coleoptera. Most of all, he worries about his family.

"Four, five, six . . ."

"Cooper, I mean it," Caddie says.

He lowers his voice. "Seven, eight, nine . . ." One at a time, That Boy turns the dollar bill faces upward. Toward the sky.

"Cooper!"

That Boy has plugged Cooper's ears. He can barely hear Caddie.

And now he matches the edges. Makes the dollar bills look neat and happy like the pages of a closed book. "Ten, eleven, twelve . . ." George Washington, smiling. Smiling and smiling. He wishes he could smile like George Washington. Without a care in the world. Twenty-seven times.

Cooper's mother stands with heavy plates in her arms, watching The Father watch That Boy.

"For God's sake," The Father says, pulling the bills from Cooper's fingers. He shoves the wad of money into the hands of the Piping Hot Pizza driver and slams the door. He wishes he would have had a twenty. "I wish, just once . . ." but he does not tell them what else he wishes. He just shakes his head with mad on his face.

Cooper's mother sets the plates on the table. Serves him two big slices of pepperoni pizza. The cheese slides to his plate and steam rises in a hot pizza cloud as she sits down. Cooper picks off the piping hot pepperoni. Stacks it on his plate like the Leaning Tower of Pisa.

"I think I'll take the kids to the cabin," she says as she tucks her long dark hair behind her ears with both hands. "I think it'll be good for them."

The cabin? Cooper carefully balances the last piece of pepperoni on the top of the tower. He doesn't want to go to the cabin. No one has been there in almost two years. Not since Grandpa died. Fell into the water and died. Reached for the fishing rod. Dropped his pipe. Burned his shirt and died.

Under the table, Cooper slides his notebook from his pocket. Holds it in his lap so no one will see what he is writing.

> Bad memories are like scary movies.
> You never forget them.

"Sounds good to me," The Father says.

"For the whole summer," Cooper's mother says.

Cooper can feel That Boy getting closer. Like a dark shadow moving across him. He freezes, except for his right foot. His right foot taps three times so softly no one can hear him. Not even The Father.

"You can't be serious," Caddie says. "You can't make me go for the whole summer. There's no TV. No running water. I'll lose my mind."

Cooper knows better than to say such a thing. Not Caddie. She is fifteen and a half years old already. His mother can't believe it. Cooper can. Cooper listens carefully as he writes in his notebook.

Everything Caddie says is getting more and more believable every day.

"I am serious," his mother says. She has mad in her voice, just like Caddie, but she is not angry. "We'll leave first thing in the morning," she says.

Caddie slams her glass of milk on the table.

Caddie will lose her mind at the cabin. His mother will lose her mind too, but only if she doesn't go. And she cannot go alone. Cannot bear to be any more alone than she is right now. But his mother doesn't say a word about her empty heart and why she must go.

Cooper understands this kind of secret. He makes another note in the notebook in his lap.

Scared sounds like angry when scared is a secret.

"It's barbaric!" Caddie screeches. "There's nothing to do. I'll die of boredom."

Cooper looks up at Caddie. Wonders if dying of boredom is truly possible.

"You can always go into town," their mother says.

"Town? It's nothing but a tourist trap. You blink once and you miss it."

"Knock it off, Caddie. You're going and that's that," The Father says.

Caddie is as angry as The Father. She leaves the table and her last piece of Piping Hot Pizza and runs upstairs. Slams her door.

Cooper stays by his mother. Everyone says he has her dark brown hair and her dark brown eyes. Do his eyes look desperate too?

"I think my dad would want us to enjoy ourselves up there," his mother says, putting Caddie's last piece of pepperoni pizza on Cooper's plate.

"Yes, Ellen, I'm sure he would," The Father says.

Don't think about Grandpa. Don't think about Grandpa. Don't think about Grandpa.

Except sometimes Cooper dreams about him. He dreams he is swimming. He dreams he hears Grandpa laughing. Laughing at their private joke about the big one that got away. He dreams the water is pink from the sunset and the cool sand is melted ice cream. But it is just a dream. When he wakes up shivering, he knows he will never go in the water. Never, ever again.

No matter what.

But he has go to the cabin. Caddie and his mother will need him. He must go. He must be brave and protect them at all costs.

Now Cooper wishes himself invisible. He stacks all of Caddie's pepperoni on his tower and takes a bite of the crust. He can feel That Boy leaning over his shoulder. He chews one, two, three times on the right side. Turns his head so no one will notice. Chews one, two, three times on the left side.

"Just once, for God's sake . . ." The Father says, slamming his hand on the table.

Cooper cringes. Stops chewing. Knows he should be more careful.

The Leaning Tower of Pisa sways and then topples, crashing into the Arno River of melted cheese. Cooper must rebuild it.

His mother stacks the dirty plates, watching The Father watch That Boy. Again.

"Just once I wish you could eat like a normal person. Something."

So does Cooper. But the medicines don't work. The doctors don't work. Happy thoughts don't work. Nothing works. That Boy won't leave him alone.

"And for the last time, put that stupid notebook away."

Cooper looks down. Pushes the notebook into his pocket.

The Father stands up suddenly with his glass of wine in one hand and a spot of orange pizza sauce on his tie. When he shoves his chair against the table, it sounds like another slammed door.

"David, please . . . ," Cooper's mother says, her eyes more desperate than ever.

"Please what? I'm tired of pussyfooting around this house like nothing's wrong."

"Cooper, why don't you go upstairs," she says softly. "Maybe you could start packing. Bring your most important things. I'll take care of your clothes."

Cooper goes upstairs. The light under Caddie's door is as straight as a laser beam. Her voice whispers. She is not packing. She is talking on her phone.

They are leaving first thing in the morning.

He must pack his most important things. His prized possessions.

He packs three small notebooks and three short number 2 pencils with sharp points and his favorite dictionary because he must write everything down. And because someday he might write a good and famous book. He packs his calendar so he does not lose track of time, and he packs his magnifying glass because there will be many things at the cabin he will have to watch closely.

He packs four of his smooth rocks, his family of rocks: one the size of his fist, two the size of cardinal eggs, and one little one, as small as a nickel. He leaves the biggest, darkest rock on his desk. Alone.

Thoop-uhzz.

Another June bug hits the window screen. Cooper stares and stares at the screen until it blurs into nothingness. He remembers the night at the cabin when Grandpa built a bonfire and told stories. The night Caddie hollered, "Cooper ate a June bug!" But he didn't. Not really. He just held the coleopteran inside his mouth and let its six sticky legs tickle his tongue. And then he tiptoed up to Caddie when she wasn't looking and set the beetle on her bare shoulder. "Cooper!" she screamed before she chased him around the fire and into the cold lake water and tickled him and made him laugh.

But that was almost two years ago. When Grandpa was still alive. When Cooper could laugh without a care in the world.

He pulls out his notebook, cups it in his hand.

Never laugh.
Laughing makes you forget what you are doing and you can never, ever, forget.

The June bug lets go. Lands on its back on the windowsill. Arms and legs reaching. Reaching and reaching. Cooper raises the screen.

Tonight he will not get a canning jar. Will not punch holes in its lid. Because even if you add grass and leaves, the June bug will die and there's nothing you can do about that except never, ever put a June bug in a canning jar. He turns the bug right side up. Scoots him off the ledge. Sends him fleeing into the night.

Amicus hiccups behind him.

"Of course I'm taking you with me," he says, so Amicus won't worry.

But he can't pack Amicus. Amicus needs to breathe. He is an amphibian. First he was an egg. Then he was an embryo. When he was a tadpole,

Cooper spotted him swimming in the bait can. "Look, Grandpa. That minnow has black dots."

"Well, well, my boy," Grandpa said with his pipe in his mouth. "That's not a minnow. The Latin name for that little guy is *rana clamitans*. You take care of that tadpole and you'll have yourself a nice little friend."

Cooper cupped his hands around the tadpole. Saved him from the gnawing minnows. "Grandpa, how do you say *friend* in Latin?"

"Amicus," Grandpa said.

"How do you do, Amicus?" Cooper said, nose to nose with the tadpole.

When Grandpa came home with the aquarium, Cooper filled it with six inches of water. And then he went outside and found a small rock on the beach, a rock the size of a nickel, and added it to his family of rocks. Like magic, Amicus grew legs and a long tongue and turned into a frog.

Cooper places one food nugget on the big plastic lily pad. Waits. Watches. Amicus jumps from his tree branch into his bowl of water. Snaps the food nugget with his long tongue.

And now Caddie, Cooper, their mother, and Amicus are going to the cabin.

For the whole summer.

But Cooper does not pack his good and famous book, *Inferno*, by Dante. Not yet. Not yet because he must keep reading the longest poem he has ever seen. So long it has chapters called cantos. It is the most important thing he will bring to the cabin.

If Caddie asks, "Why are you reading that?" he will tell her it is a good and famous book.

He will tell her it is a classic. And he will tell her it is a must-read for everyone.

He will not tell her he stole it from Grandpa's suitcase when the ambulance was gone and they packed up all of Grandpa's things to go home. He will not tell her that it smells like Grandpa's pipe tobacco. Or that *inferno* means "fire." That if he misses the third word or the third line or the third page, everyone he loves will go up in flames.

We, we, we. In, in, in. Our, our, our . . . We in our turn stepped forward toward the city and through the gate . . .

Cooper reads the perfect words perfectly. Reads and reads. He reads into the night as if his life depends on it.

Because it does.

FLEEING

It's not first thing in the morning. It's three nineteen in the afternoon. "Caddie! Cooper!" We need to get going!"

With careful hands, Cooper touches goodbye to his bed and the desk and its seven knobs and the lamp and the puppets and the truck and the empty hangers in his closet, one by one, and the big rock and all the things he knows he will leave behind.

Caddie's door is open. She is still packing. She packs two bathing suits, check. Ten pairs of socks, check. Eleven pairs of underwear, check. And then she turns around. "Get out of my room, Cooper."

Cooper lugs his backpack down the stairs to the kitchen. When he sets his backpack on the kitchen table next to the spices and cereal boxes and toilet paper, the thud is as loud as a hammer against cement.

His mother moves the backpack to the floor. "Whoa! What have you got in this thing?" she asks. "Rocks?"

Cooper nods quickly and then he shakes his head. He pulls his notebook from his pocket. Leans on the kitchen table.

Sometimes it is hard to tell the difference between secrets and truth.

When he goes upstairs to get Amicus, he passes Caddie coming down the stairs with her suitcase. Bump, bump, bump . . .

The aquarium is heavy. Cooper wraps his arms around the cool glass, carries it into the kitchen. "Don't tell me you're bringing that stupid frog to the cabin," Caddie says. "There's a million of them up there as it is." She moves a stack of towels to make room on the counter.

"Amicus depends on me," he says, setting the aquarium next to the ketchup, mustard, and pickles.

"But what if we get confused and think he's a hamburger?" Caddie picks up the ketchup bottle, lifts a corner of the screen cover, and pretends to squirt ketchup all over the frog.

"Oh, Caddie," their mother says.

"Nuh-uh," Cooper says, pinching the screen tight at the corner. He knows Caddie would never do such a thing.

When their mother says, "Bring me the ivy," Caddie gets the miniature fishing boat made of glass and filled with dirt. A gift from the neighbors for Grandpa's funeral. It will break if Caddie drops it. Break and shatter their mother's heart into a million pieces. "Dad won't bother with this while we're gone."

"He won't bother with anything," Caddie says.

"Oh, Caddie," their mother says again, but Cooper believes what Caddie says.

"You can be in charge of watering the plants at the cabin, Cooper." His mother pats him on his shoulder. "Once a week."

"You mean *plant*," he says.

"Maybe we'll get more," she says.

"Okay," he says. He will water the ivy once a week. He knows it will not die because it is already dead. He turns the page of his notebook.

Living things do not die twice.

You only have one chance and then it is over and there is nothing you can do about it.

Cooper knows the ivy is dead because he has examined it closely with his magnifying glass. There are no leaves dangling from the pot the way they did at Grandpa's funeral. And sticky green tape wound around a piece of wire is not a living thing. But his mother has put all her hope in this little pot, so he will keep the very important dead ivy a secret too.

"We need to load the van," his mother says.

Cooper carries groceries down the sidewalk. One trip, two trips, three trips. He carries Amicus to the van last.

"Packing takes forever," Caddie says, following him with an armload of pillows and blankets.

Amicus will ride on top of Caddie's suitcase next to Cooper. Next to the dead ivy. "Is that so he can see out?" his mother asks. No. Amicus rides high so Cooper can see into his aquarium. Make sure his three-chamber heart beats. Beats and beats, pushing his cold blood through his veins. *Beat. Beat. Beat.* The frog's body throbs. Blood rushes away, rushes back. Travels in a circle. There is no stopping it. Unless you are dead.

"Hey, Cooper," Caddie says from the front seat. "You want to play 'I Spy'?"

Cooper shakes his head. "No. Thank you," he says.

"C'mon, Coop. It'll be fun. Like old times."

But it won't be like old times. Looking out the windows and finding colors of things they see flashing by won't be fun. It will mean reading the signs and the billboards three times three and he won't be able to keep up because they go by so quickly and he might be risking everyone's lives if he can't keep up.

What if they have a car accident? What if they hit a raccoon trying to cross the road? Or a whole family of raccoons? What if something else happens? Something he hasn't thought of? No, he won't play 'I Spy.' He will read his good and famous book.

"Cooper?"

"I'm reading," he says.

At dusk, they stop for fast food. Cooper sets the aquarium in the center of the table where they eat outside and gives Amicus one food nugget. *Don't, don't, don't*, he thinks to himself, but he can't help it. It's That Boy. That Boy follows him everywhere. Like a shadow. Cooper chews each bite of his hamburger three times on each side, turning his face so no one will notice. And then they get ice cream. His favorite.

"How much longer?" Caddie says.

"About another hundred miles," their mother says.

Cooper reaches for his book. His good and famous book. North is the direction they drive as Cooper reads. Reads and reads. On his left the red sun sits heavy in the sky, taunting, like a bomb. As if it will explode when it hits the horizon. Darkness waits its turn on his right.

"We'll have a lot of work to do," his mother says as she drives. "I'll need your help. We'll have to clean and make the beds and wash the dishes . . ."

Cooper lets his mother's voice go free, like the wind. Like the buzzing of insects, and thinks how happy Amicus would be to catch one of her words in the air with his tongue. Except for that one word. *Dad.* That one word stops everything. "Dad will come up after work on Fridays and stay for the weekend."

Worries bounce through Cooper's mind like hopping toads. His thoughts land on the dark, smooth rock he has left at home on his desk. The family of rocks is not together. When The Father comes to the cabin, the big rock will be at home. Alone.

Cooper hears The Father's voice booming, "Stop that before you embarrass yourself. I mean it. Right now." He wishes he had a big rock for That Boy. Wishes he could have left That Boy at home on his desk. Alone.

Boom. The sun has landed and it is dark.

Now Cooper reads with his flashlight. *Why. Why. Why. Do. Do. Do. You. You. You. Squander? Squander? Squander? Why do you squander . . .*

For ninety-seven miles Cooper reads. Reads and reads. Reads until the van slows and turns, driving deeper into the blackness beneath the giant pine trees. Branches crack under the tires. The engine sputters and stops. Caddie lifts her head from her pillow. Amicus lifts his head above the water toward the beam of the flashlight. Fireflies pop on and off in the tall grass like blinking cat eyes.

They have arrived safe and sound. No one has burst into flames. Cooper wants to shout: *My mother and sister are alive! Amicus is alive too!* But he knows they won't understand.

He shuts off his flashlight and leans over the aquarium. "Listen," he says. In the dark he writes this down:

Sometimes you can hear everything when you can't hear anything.

The northern air is cool. The trees are silhouettes against the blue-black sky. Caddie pulls on the screen door of the cabin. It squeaks open. Cooper would know that squeak anywhere. It belongs only to this old door in the woods. His mother unlocks the heavy cabin door, pushes into the blackness. Whispers, "It still smells like his pipe." Cooper knows she has tears in her eyes, but it is too dark to see them.

Sometimes you cannot see things that are crystal clear.

His mother pulls open the curtains. The bright moonbeam reaches across the lake and into the cabin with a long finger of white light.

The cabin is like a museum. All things are still and lifeless. The sofa and the chairs and the two kerosene lamps on the mantel and the mouse trap behind the broom and the pots and the pans and the salt and pepper shakers and Grandpa's leaping-trout keyring, the one with his initials, PM, on the hook by the back door.

Cooper feels a shiver. Then a tremble. He imagines himself as the lake with a rumbling motorboat moving through him.

Nothing at the cabin has been touched in almost two whole years.

That Boy must touch it all.

He touches the doorknob and the four corners of the desk. He touches the big nails in Grandpa's leather chair by the fireplace, one by one.

Caddie turns on a light. The pine walls glow golden. Everything lurks in the shadows. Now That Boy must touch the lampshade and the old-fashioned phone and the curls in its cord. One, two, three . . . until Cooper feels his mother's sad dark eyes. He hides the cord behind his back, touching and counting as fast as he can, parting his lips so she will think he is smiling. Happy and smiling, so she will forget how sad she is at the cabin knowing Grandpa is gone. Dead. Nothing you can do about it now.

"It's cold in here," Caddie says. "Can we build a fire?"

A fire? Terror shoots through Cooper. Alerts every nerve. Stops his breath.

"No, I think it's too late for that," his mother says.

Cooper breathes again.

"Cooper," his mother says, "I have just the job for you. Caddie and I will make the beds—"

"Wait a minute," Caddie says. "I'm not sharing a room with him anymore."

Cooper's mother blinks in slow motion. Looks around the golden cabin. "I guess there's Grandpa's room," she says.

Grandpa's room. Grandpa's room. Grandpa's room. Grandpa's room is a safe place. Like a base camp. Cooper will be the sentry guard. "I'll sleep in Grandpa's room," Cooper says. "I'm the man of the house."

"Okay," his mother says, trying to smile. "Can the man of the house bring in the groceries?"

The groceries are a big and important job. Food is sustenance. Food gives life. Cooper nods. Yes, he can bring in the groceries. He will bring in the groceries to make his mother happy.

The cereal boxes and chips and cookies fit into place on the open shelves like puzzle pieces. Soup cans and salt and cinnamon and many other red-capped spices are stacked in perfect rows. The groceries are snug and safe, like ancient cliff dwellings packed into the mesa. Everything fits. And it is beautiful.

"Cooper, what in the world . . .?" His mother says.

"Geez, Cooper," Caddie says.

His mother squeezes Caddie's hand to keep her quiet. Smiles at Cooper. He sees her think he doesn't know. Sees her pretend everything is okay and he aches with this lie.

"Thank you, Cooper. You've done a good job. Now it's time for bed. Use the bathroom and brush your teeth."

"There is no bathroom," Cooper says.

"Don't be difficult," Caddie says. "You know what she means."

"Okay," he says. He will be good. He will do everything he can to be good. He grabs his flashlight and runs to the outhouse at the edge of the woods. The ground is cold and the small door opens with a tiny squeak. The outhouse is good for the environment. The outhouse saves water.

When Cooper runs back into the cabin, Caddie is in the kitchen in her polar bear pajamas. He pulls on the pump handle at the sink. The bolt screeches. The water trickles brown and thin and smells like rotten eggs. He holds his breath. Steps back.

"Cooper, watch," Caddie says. She pumps the pump with both hands, up and down, with all her might. The pump brays like a donkey. "Watch," she says again and squirts toothpaste on her toothbrush, holds it under pale yellow water. She brushes her teeth, pumping the handle with one hand until the water turns clear. "You just have to get it going," she says. Bubbling toothpaste spit rolls down her chin and she smiles at him and says, "See," and something else he can't understand because the toothbrush is still in her mouth.

"What?"

"Your turn," she says, spitting one more time. "I'll pump the water."

Caddie pumps and pumps. The donkey brays. Cooper copies Caddie, up and down, and turns away. Up and down, three times three, first the top teeth, and then the bottom teeth, and then the insides, breathing through his mouth, one, two, three . . .

"Would you hurry up?" she says. "Please? I don't have all day."

Caddie is already losing her mind at the cabin, so he hurries to spit in the kitchen sink. The white spit spirals down the drain and seeps into the earth with the worms and the water bugs and into the ground-water and travels all the way to Louisiana and on to Mexico where someone drinks his toothpaste spit and he is definitely sure brushing his teeth is not a good thing to do to the world.

"Good night, Cooper, Caddie," their mother says.

"Good night," Cooper says. Caddie has already closed her bedroom door.

Cooper carries Amicus to Grandpa's old bedroom. Puts the aquarium on the dresser Grandpa built from smooth pine boards as golden as the walls. He moves the old black-and-white photo of the lake at sunset so Amicus can see it and opens the food jar. Amicus gets one food nugget at bedtime. *Plop.* "You're a good frog," Cooper says.

He puts his flashlight and his good and famous book under his pillow. Hangs his calendar from a hook on the wall. Places a checkmark on June first. Eighty-six days to go.

One by one, he lays out his smooth rocks next to Amicus's aquarium. One big one, two medium ones, and the little one, the size of a nickel. He changes into his warm pajamas and sits on the edge of his bed. On Grandpa's red wool blanket with the big black stripe. He runs his finger between each of his toes. Lets the sand fall to the floor. Then he turns off the light and crawls under the blanket. Lies back on his lumpy pillow. He breathes the air his grandfather breathed. Watches the moon his grandfather watched. Wishes he could make this room whole again. He slides *Inferno* and his flashlight from under his pillow.

Fire in his hands.

Breaths quiver deep inside him, shaking their way up and out of his ribcage. *We. We. We. In. In. In. Our. Our. Our . . . We in our turn stepped forward toward the city and through the gate . . .*

Between the words, in the midst of quick breaths, a sudden noise. The noise comes from Amicus. Just like Cooper read in Grandpa's book on North American wildlife, Amicus sounds like someone gulping and gulping. Amicus is croaking with gulping breaths. Amicus is happy to be at the cabin in the dark woods.

Not Cooper. The cabin is sad without Grandpa, and the dark lake is scary, and there is a lot to keep track of.

He gets out of bed. Shines the flashlight on the aquarium and stands eye-to-eye with Amicus. "Does it smell like home?" he whispers. The croaking stops, so he gets back into bed. He has six hundred and ninety-three words, ninety-nine lines, and three more pages to go so the Earth and Amicus and his sister and his mother and The Father and even That Boy will not burst into flames.

SANDCASTLES

Cooper pours the cinnamon into a small bowl and keeps the jar. He grabs two soup cans from the garbage and the red cleaning bucket from under the sink. He carries his building supplies to the beach.

If you dig deep enough, you can find wet sand. Wet sand is cold and solid and stays where you put it. Tomato soup cans make the best molds for towers, but empty spice jars make good turrets. When the castle is done, it will sparkle like the great city of Oz in the distance beyond the poppy field.

Cooper, the mighty warrior, digs his fingers into the sand like a backhoe. A deep moat will protect his people and avert fires that might crop up out of nowhere.

A loon howls across the lake. The waves lap at the shore. In between, Cooper hears the click of flip-flops.

An enemy is approaching.

He must stay low.

The sound stops above him at the top of the hill. "Have you been here the whole time?"

Cooper stands up. Caddie's blond hair glows in the sunlight. Caddie is not the enemy. She is a fellow warrior. With worry in her voice. He nods.

"Didn't you hear us calling? You know you're not supposed to come down to the beach by yourself." Now she has mad in her voice.

"I'd never go swimming by myself," Cooper says. He looks at the dark boathouse sitting at the edge of the lake. The house for Grandpa's boat. Its gray shadow cast across the sand. He hears the water lapping at the dead reeds. Dead. Just like Grandpa.

Don't think. Don't think. Don't think. Cooper knows he would never go beyond that edge. He is a rule follower. The best rule follower there is. "I am a rule follower," he says.

"Yeah, right," Caddie says. "Until you do whatever you feel like."

But Cooper knows he would never go beyond the shore into the deep water. Not the deep, black water where he jumped from the dock and splashed and examined minnows through his goggles. Where he held his breath and floated like a dead man. And he did not think about that word. *Dead*. He wishes with all his might he could play like that again. But now he is a warrior. A warrior with a code of conduct.

He touches his empty pocket. Pictures his notebook on his pillow. He must remember to write this down:

Sometimes it looks like you are breaking the rules when you are following an ancient code of conduct.

"I've been very busy," Cooper says. He picks up the red bucket and hurries to the edge of the lake. Stands ankle deep in the safe yellow foam and rotting weeds and fills the bucket to its brim. He walks slowly, so he won't spill, and pours the lake water into the moat. As fast as he pours it, the water seeps into the darkened sand and disappears. He gets another bucket of water. Splashes his feet as he hurries. Pours the water into the moat. The water disappears again.

The Earth has a big hole in it.

"Cooper," Caddie says, coming down the hill.

"What?"

"Give me the bucket." Caddie sighs a sigh as deep as a hole dug to China. "And find me some leaves to line the moat, so the water stays put. I'll get the water. You hurry."

Cooper runs off with an eye to the ground for leaves. He steps on pine needles and acorns and sandy grass. Almost steps on a little gray toad. He thinks of Amicus and how badly Amicus would like to swim in a real lake when he grows up, so he hikes toward the cabin.

"Green leaves!" Caddie shouts as he rounds the top of the hill.

"The greenest leaves!" he hollers back.

The screen door squeaks open. Snaps shut. "Wipe your feet!" his mother calls. "Dad's coming and you know how he likes things just so."

Cooper is already wiping his feet. First one foot, and then the other foot. *Just so. Just so. Just so.*

Amicus sees him coming and lifts his head. Cooper gives him an extra food nugget so the frog will have extra strength to swim in the moat. And he waits. He waits for the food nugget to dissolve in Amicus's belly because he has read in a book how dangerous it is to swim on a full stomach.

He waits and waits and waits.

He puts his small notebook and one small pencil in his pocket while he counts to two hundred and forty. Then he scoops Amicus from his aquarium with a plastic dish, microwave safe, covers it with a strainer, and carries Amicus out of the cabin and down the hill to his private beach and sandcastle in the sun.

"What took so long?" Caddie asks.

"Amicus wanted to come with me."

Caddie shakes her head. She is mad again. She has found a hundred leaves, all by herself, and has plastered them against the moat walls and filled the moat with water.

She is a good warrior.

The moat drains more slowly, but it is almost empty. Amicus won't have enough time to swim before every last drop is gone.

"Why do you even need a moat?" Caddie asks.

"To defend the castle against the enemy. And to avoid fires."

"Can't you just pretend?"

"I am."

Caddie frowns. "I have an idea." She brushes the sand from her hands. "I'll be right back," she says, and runs up the hill toward the cabin.

Cooper places Amicus on the ground, in the shade of the birch tree. He pulls his small notebook from his pocket and sets it next to Amicus's dish. "You stay put," he says, and then he fills the red bucket with lake water and pours it into the moat one, two, three times. For a nanosecond, the moat is full to the brim. He thinks of the dead ivy from Grandpa's funeral in its little glass boat and his mother watching the green tape, waiting for the leaves to return, and he knows that what he feels for this tiny second is hope.

And then he hears a laugh.

Two big, tanned boys in shorts are walking up the beach, tapping thick sticks like canes, swinging giant plastic ice cream buckets. They pass the boathouse at the edge of the water. Pause. Scan the ground. Poke under the dock with their sticks.

The tallest boy picks up a rock and throws it across the lake. It touches down one, two, three times. The boy with blond hair and a big smile that never goes away can top that one, easy. He picks up a rock, winds up like a pitcher, and sends the rock across the top of the water like a hovercraft. The rock touches down one, two, three, four times. The boys laugh. The blond boy slaps the dark-haired boy on his back. They must have a private joke between them.

But they are strangers. And they are getting closer every second.

And then they see Cooper.

"Do you live here?" asks the tall boy with dark hair and pimples all over his face. He points his stick up the hill toward the cabin.

Cooper shakes his head and shivers and holds the empty red bucket to his stomach with both hands. No one lives here. It's just a cabin. He and his mother and Caddie and Amicus are on vacation. And That Boy is standing right next to him.

"Are you just here for the summer?" Tall Boy asks.

Cooper takes a deep breath. Nods. "I'm here for seventy-nine more days."

"So you're one of those. A city boy," says the other boy, the blond one with smooth skin like the boys in Caddie's magazines. He pokes his stick in the sand. Leans on it. Grins.

That Boy doesn't like that grin.

"We thought this place was abandoned," Tall Boy says.

"Yeah. Abandoned. Like we could burn it down and no one would ever know," the blond grinner says.

Burn it down. Burn it down. Burn it down. Cooper's nerves sputter. He trembles from the inside out.

"What's your name?" Tall Boy asks.

"C-c-ooper." He shivers more, wishing with all his might Caddie will come down the hill. He looks over his shoulder. She is not coming down the hill. She is not coming right back. He looks at his sandcastle. At the draining moat. He wishes the lake were a great circle of moat around the cabin. But it is just a lake. And now he is glad Caddie is not coming down the hill. She would not be safe. And he is glad That Boy is standing next to him.

That Boy slaps Cooper on the back.

Cooper can't help himself. Does not want to help himself. Wants to help everyone. He stomps the ground one, two, three times with his left foot. Feels every grain of sand sift through the hairs on his shin. He stomps the ground one, two, three times with his right foot.

"What's with you?" The Grinner says.

Go away. Go away. Go away. Cooper thinks these words. Feels them tumble through his brain. Sees them fall into a gulley in his skull. The words are drowning. Cooper cannot reach them. Cannot save his drowning words.

He says no words at all.

"We're just trying to make friends," Tall Boy says.

"Yeah," says The Grinner. "Friends. But if you can't be friendly, I'll just have to do THIS." The Grinner whacks the sandcastle with his stick. The turret of Oz explodes in the sunlight. A billion dazzling crystals. The Grinner laughs.

The moat has failed.

The enemy has breached the castle walls.

"Whadja do that for?" Tall Boy asks. "He's just a kid. C'mon." Tall Boy runs with long legs, like a frog's. "C'mon!" he hollers to The Grinner. "You want his mom or dad after us or something?"

The Grinner whoops. Chases after Tall Boy. Chases him as far as the birch tree. Trips over Amicus's dish. Knocks the strainer and Amicus into the sand. Then The Grinner stops. Stops and leers over Amicus.

Cooper freezes. Hugs his red bucket.

"What's this?" The Grinner says. "Frog legs for lunch?" He raises his stick like a spear. Amicus raises his head. Looks The Grinner in the eye.

"Todd! C'mon!" Tall Boy yells from the neighbor's dock.

The Grinner grins. Aims. "Ready, set . . ."

Cooper watches The Grinner's stick blur to nothingness.

"Todd!" Tall Boy runs back. Grabs The Grinner by the arm. The spear releases. *Thwup!* The spear sways side to side, nose-down in the sand.

The Grinner sneers at Tall Boy. "You made me miss!"

"Leave him alone and c'mon. I'll be late for work." Tall Boy runs again.

The Grinner picks up the stick and looks at Cooper. For a second, the grin is only in his eyes, and then his teeth begin to show. He kicks the sand, and Cooper's little notebook flutters across the beach like a giant paper moth. He shoots Cooper another grin and kicks the microwave-safe dish into the air. It drops into the sand at Cooper's feet.

Another grin.

Amicus is next.

Cooper takes a deep breath.

But Amicus outsmarts The Grinner. In an instant, the frog leaps and lands in the dead and rotting weeds on the shore.

Cooper sighs.

The Grinner grins. Turns away. Catches up to Tall Boy. Together The Grinner and Tall Boy run up the beach, swinging their buckets.

Cooper hurries to the shore. Drops to his knees in the reeds. Scoops Amicus into his hands. "I'm sorry," he says. He wishes he would have yelled at the boys. Wishes he could have grabbed a stick and chased them. Knows The Father would never go after Tall Boy and The Grinner. Would only yell at Cooper. Cooper wishes he would have yelled The Father's words, "What's wrong with you?"

Cowards and chickens and sissies do not climb over docks with big, tanned boys. They can't skip rocks. They can't run with long legs, like a frog, without a care in the world. And they would never raise their heads bravely toward the spear.

Amicus is brave.

Amicus is a hero.

"From now on you will be known as Amicus the Great."

Cooper refills the microwave-safe dish, puts Amicus the Great inside, and covers the bowl with the strainer. He sets the dish in the shade of the birch tree. Brushes the sand from his notebook. Stares at a blank and dirty page and thinks to himself, *Sometimes writing down nothing is better than writing down something.*

Amicus was in danger, and Cooper did nothing. Said nothing. Leaving the page blank will remind him of the close call. And how he is a coward. He writes

June 8th

on the blank and dirty page so he never forgets he did nothing. *Nothing, nothing, nothing.* He puts the notebook in his pocket. Picks up a rock. Throws it at the lake. The rock does not skip one, two, three, four times. It hides beneath the water. Like a coward. Like Cooper. He pulls out his notebook one more time.

From now on I will try to be as strong and brave as Amicus the Great.

Cooper returns to Oz. The castle walls have crumbled. The towers are flattened. Cooper will have to start over. Build a castle bigger and better than Oz. Create a new and safe world for all creatures. Where heroes live forever. He stomps on what is left of the turret. Stomps with all his might. Stomps until the sandcastle melts into the beach.

"Cooper!" Caddie yells. "Cooper, Cooper,

Cooper," she says, but every time she says his name it sounds like it is dropping off the edge of a cliff. To its death. Cooper knows he has failed her.

She shakes her head and holds up a long yellow box of plastic wrap. "I don't understand you," she whispers with mean in her voice and maybe sadness too. She has had it. She cannot take another step. She sits down. Slaps the long yellow box on the ground. Kicks at the sand.

Now the plastic wrap is ruined too.

"Why did you do that? It was beautiful. I told you I had an idea." Caddie shakes her head again, her mouth open, the words shocked out of it. Her eyes are wide and shiny and Cooper knows she has seen a ghost. A ghost of Cooper. A ghost of a secret. She has not seen the truth.

"If you just would have waited. Mom needed me to help her . . ." She unrolls a little plastic wrap from the box. Waves the box in the air. "I think this would have worked." She stands, brushes off her shorts, and goes back up the hill. The plastic wrap sparkles in the air, waving like an invisible flag.

Caddie has not surrendered.

She has given up.

There is a difference.

Please come back. Please, please, please. Cooper wants to tell Caddie about Tall Boy and The Grinner. Tell her his secret. But he cannot. He does not want to frighten her. He must protect her at all costs. Cannot ever fail her again.

"Better get Amicus out of the sun before he explodes," Caddie says from the top of the hill. She does not look back. "And you better come eat some breakfast."

Amicus the Great! The sun has shifted. The dish is hot. Amicus is under water to keep cool. Cooper is there in the nick of time.

He carries the frog up the hill and across the yard and into the cabin to the safety of the dresser in his cool, dark room. He pours Amicus into his swimming dish with a silent splash.

"Cooper!" his mother yells from the kitchen. "Wipe your feet. Dad called and he can't make it this weekend, but I still want the place kept clean."

Yes, he will wipe his feet. He will wipe, wipe, wipe his feet. And then he will wipe his feet again. He stomps his left foot one, two, three times. Then the right foot. He hears The Father's words: *Stop that right now before you embarrass yourself.* But he cannot stop. He stomps his feet again. That Boy knows

Amicus had a close call. That Boy will never let him forget how close he came to disaster.

He pushes his fingers between his toes and lets the sand fall to the floor. He brushes and brushes and brushes the sand away until his feet are raw and his toes burn like fire and he cannot brush them anymore.

He thinks of the big, dark rock at home on his desk, alone. Thinks of the two tanned boys. He grabs his good and famous book and climbs onto his bed.

The cabin is not a sandcastle. It cannot be kicked into thin air. But it could catch fire and burn. Cooper imagines the lake is a great moat around the cabin. No sticks. No strangers. No fires.

He reads. Reads and reads. He reads to save Amicus from the cruel world.

Poor, brave Amicus.

Cooper pulls his notebook from his pocket and turns the page.

Heroes never die, but they can be killed.

There is a difference.

WORDS

Rain pours straight and steady from the sky like prison bars. The cabin windows are open, but the air is the same inside and outside. Warm and soggy. Caddie shuffles her deck of cards. "Could you get your snotty nose out of that book for one minute and join the real world?"

Caddie does not know the truth about books.

Books are real. Powerfully real. More powerful than their words.

More powerful than anyone can imagine.

"You shouldn't be reading it anyway. It's too old for you. No wonder it's taking you so long."

Cooper touches his nose. "My nose is not snotty."

"Geez, Cooper. It's just a saying."

Caddie slaps the deck of cards on the end table. Two days of rain in a row and she has bored herself silly with games of solitaire. Now she is filing her fingernails.

Cooper likes the rain. He writes this down,

Rain is reliable. Rain calms the world. Turns it all one color.

The sky is gray, the air is gray, the lake is gray. When it is raining, everyone stays in the cabin. In the big golden room, together. Safe and sound. Cooper likes knowing where everyone is. And wet things do not burn. Not very well anyway.

Still, he must be on constant alert. He reads with his eyes, not his ears.

Gray thunder rumbles across the gray lake. The rasp of Caddie's nail file stops. She sighs. His mother's knitting needles tat-tat together, pause. Tat-tat, pause.

"When is it supposed to clear up?" Caddie asks. She turns on a lamp by her chair.

"I think they predicted rain all day," their mother says. Tat-tat, pause.

Cooper picks up his pencil.

Predicting the weather is like predicting the future. It is impossible. One tiny drop of rain changes everything.

"I think I have cabin fever," Caddie says.

"You could try reading," their mother says. She sits by the stone fireplace, knitting a yellow and white striped afghan for a neighbor's baby. She does not sit in the big leather chair. Does not sit in Grandpa's chair where he read the newspaper and his books and smoked his pipe.

"Maybe you could play a game with me, Coop," Caddie says, getting up and plopping down next to him on the sofa, filing her nails again.

Cooper doesn't answer. Does not want to lose count of his words.

"I could teach you to knit," their mother says.

"I'd rather die first," Caddie says.

Die.

That word stops Cooper's eyes in their tracks. He presses his pointer finger tight to the page and looks up. Watches Caddie closely for signs of death. She is still breathing. Her eyes blink. Lime-green fingernail dust falls to her lap. She is still alive.

"C'mon, Cooper. One game. Like Monopoly.

Besides, you'll go blind if you don't turn on a light."

Cooper looks back at his book. Lifts his finger to see the next word: *lantern*. Reading this word when Caddie tells him to turn on a light is irony. He reads the word two more times and knows Caddie's words to be true. It is hard to see in the dim light on a rainy day. He could go blind. Does not want to go blind. There are too many things he must watch closely.

"Monopoly takes longer than a minute," he says.

"Of course it does," Caddie says. "So what if it takes the rest of the day? That book will still be there."

That book will still be there. That book will still be there. That book will still be there. That is the problem. That Book is like That Boy. It won't go away. Won't leave him alone. And Cooper is getting tired. He is afraid the fiery orange book will last forever and he won't have the strength to finish it. Caddie has rescued him. As if swept to shore by a great wave, he takes a deep breath. He would like more than anything to play a game.

Cooper closes his book. "I'll get the board." He crosses the room to the tall cedar armoire, the antique cabinet Grandpa found by the side of the road. He opens the creaky doors. The games are stacked on the shelves.

Everything in the armoire smells sweet. Like moldy bread. But Monopoly is not there with the other games, like Scrabble and Sorry.

"Look up," Caddie says.

Cooper looks up. Monopoly is on top of the armoire. Next to the jigsaw puzzles. Out of reach. Over his head like a dark cloud on this rainy day. A shiver runs through him. But he knows he does not have to touch the jigsaw puzzles. Does not have to worry about finding every piece and then finding every piece a place. He will not touch them.

He drags a chair to the armoire, climbs up.

"I'll play Monopoly if you play Scrabble," he says.

Caddie rolls her eyes. But she can't. Not really. It is just a saying.

"I'll play too, if you play Scrabble," their mother says, stabbing the silver knitting needles into the ball of yellow yarn.

"And then we get to play Monopoly," Caddie says.

"We have all summer," their mother says.

Caddie pushes aside the placemats and napkin holder. Cooper sets the Scrabble game on the dining room table. "We have sixty-eight days," he says.

"Don't remind me," Caddie says. She sits down in a chair and opens the box. A piece of the brown box lid dangles from yellowed tape. "This must be the first Scrabble game ever made. It's so old, it's probably in Latin."

"Sanskrit," Cooper says.

He is serious, but their mother laughs. "My mom and dad had this game forever."

Cooper hands out the wooden trays. He shakes the bag of letters and takes one. The letter T. "I have selected an alveolar."

"A what?" Caddie says.

"An alveolar." He shows Caddie the letter. "A sound made with the tip of the tongue carefully placed against the teeth. Like this: *tuh*," he says, exaggerating with his tongue. "The letter T is an alveolar."

"*Tuh*," she says with a sneer, shaking her head. She sticks her tongue out past her teeth as far as she can. "I'm not playing if you keep doing that."

"Now, Caddie," their mother says.

Caddie raises an eyebrow. She really can raise just one.

Caddie pulls the letter A from the bag. "Ha! I go first!"

"Going clockwise, you're next, Cooper," their mother says. "And I'm last."

Caddie counts out seven new letters. So

does Cooper. And their mother. Caddie spells "CEMENT," placing the N on the black star in the center of the board.

Cooper sees his play instantly: with Caddie's C he can make "ACQUIRES" and use all his letters for eighty-eight points.

"What did you get?" their mother asks.

"Twenty-six," Caddie says. As she turns the board toward Cooper, the letters of "CEMENT" shift out of line.

No, no, no. Cooper moves the C back to its little square, then the first E, then the M. Every time he touches one letter, another one moves. *No, no, no.* He imagines a fourth tray of letters right next to his. A tray for That Boy.

Caddie presses her fingertips hard on the edge of the game board. "I'll play upside down from now on," she says. "Then the pieces won't move so much."

But he can't help it. That Boy has hold of his hand. He moves the second E into its space, looks at Caddie. She smiles at him—right into his eyes—but he looks away. "Okay, Cooper?" That Boy touches the N. "Okay?" Caddie says again, mad growing in her voice like a swelling balloon, a balloon about to pop. "Please?"

But That Boy won't look at her. That Boy doesn't like to be told what to do. He puts his finger on the T. Holds it steady.

"Cooper!"

"Okay," he says, and then he lays down Q-U-I to spell "QUIT" across the end of "CEMENT" for only fourteen points because he knows how much Caddie hates to lose.

"I say we all go into town for pizza tonight," their mother says.

"Anything to get out of here," Caddie says.

They play until the rain stops and the sun hints again at daytime. They play until they are hungry. They play until Caddie spells "ZITHERS" and "SNAKES" using all her letters for fifty bonus points and the bag of letters is empty.

Cooper puts his fist to his mouth like a microphone and lowers his voice. "Here she comes. It's Caddie Girl up from behind. Making the rounds on the inner circle." He leans over his mother's shoulder and watches her tally their final scores. He thrusts his fist into the air in victory. "One hundred ninety-seven points to Mama Ellen's one hundred eighty-four points. Caddie Girl has won by a nose. And here comes Cooper Boy, bringing up the rear with one hundred and fifty-six points. It's amazing. Simply amazing. No one could have predicted such an outcome!"

Caddie laughs so hard she snorts and spit flies from her mouth. She grabs a paper napkin from the napkin holder. Their mother stands and dances in a circle. Cooper watches them, puts his hand to his mouth to stop his smile. He wants to smile, knowing Caddie and his mother can pretend it has always been like this wonderful moment. And it really, truly is like this wonderful moment.

Sometimes wonderful sneaks up on you when you're not looking.

"It's a miracle," Cooper says.

Thunder cracks. Rain pours down in sheets.

"It's raining again," Caddie says, and this time she laughs.

Until brakes squeak on the main road at the end of the driveway.

Their mother stops dancing.

Caddie turns.

Cooper looks too.

Together they watch through the small window. Through the steady gray rain.

The Father's fancy black car rolls down the driveway, winding between the trees, windshield wipers snapping back and forth, quick and angry.

Sometimes something happens so suddenly you are not prepared for the shock of ordinary things.

"I guess I better get dinner started," their mother says.

"So much for pizza," Caddie says.

Cooper drops back in his chair at the dining room table. His elbow catches on the corner of the game. Bounces the board. Tiles fly like popping corn. He hurries to put the letters back in their squares, back in line, back where they belong. Hurries to make the broken words whole again.

"It's okay, Coop," Caddie says. "The game's over. Just put them back in the bag." She scoops up a handful of letters. "That was fun," she says.

Cooper shakes his head. Their fun is nothing but a mess. A mess that makes Cooper's insides quake.

That Boy takes over, picking up the letters. Lining up the trays. Looking to the top of the armoire to put the game away.

The black car parks beneath the tall pine trees. The engine stops. Cooper hurries.

Sometimes everything starts when everything stops.

Cooper cannot put the game away without a chair to climb on.

The car door slams.

There is no time to get a chair.

Cooper jumps.

Arms overhead, both hands on the game, he jumps again. Brushes the top of the armoire with the box. Jumps with all his might. Pushes the game into place. Pushes again until the game lines up edge to edge with the top of the armoire. Until the game bumps into the stack of puzzles.

A box shifts.

Soars.

Opens.

A spray of jigsaw puzzle cascades around him. Like rain.

Like rain, one thousand machine-perfect pieces of *Flags of the World* in authentic color fall to the floor.

Outside, stiff shoes slide across the cement walk. "Damn rain," The Father says.

FAULT

For five fast breaths, the puzzle spill is beautiful. Dangerously beautiful. Like blue flames. Like sun dogs. Like hurricanes in a swirl before they strike land. Before they become chaos and panic. Before fear sets in. Before someone might trip and fall.

Or burn up.

Or get mad.

"You better hurry and pick up that mess," Caddie says.

Cooper can't move. He glances at the box, opened and upside down. Like a dead squirrel on the sidewalk. One wrong move and splat. You're dead. Nothing you can do about it.

In the rubble, he spots a dot of green. Like shrapnel. He recognizes the fragment of a cedar tree. The flag of Lebanon. Knows there is more. Another branch. A whole canopy. Cooper shudders. That Boy has already beaten him to it. That Boy will have to find the pieces. All of them. He must make the broken tree whole.

"Here," Caddie says. She hands Cooper the box with one hand, holds a clump of puzzle pieces with the other. Another handful. And another. She puts the lid on the box. On the box of broken trees, ripped flags, and shattered crests. That Boy is scared. Worried. Frustrated.

"You missed some," Cooper says, dropping to his hands and knees. Caddie takes the box. Lifts the lid.

Cooper adds three more pieces to the pile. "Set it on the dining room table. Hurry. I have to fix it."

"But Dad's here," Caddie says. "For dinner."

Dad. The Father. He likes things just so.

Just so. Just so. Just so.

"There," Cooper says, pointing at the big coffee table. "Put it there." He crawls across the floor, picking up the few remaining scattered pieces. Two fire-red shards of Japan's single-dot flag hang together. He will start with the red sun of Japan.

The screen door squeaks open. Snaps shut.

"Hi, Dad," Caddie says.

Cooper has spotted one more puzzle piece. A yellow one. Under the big coffee table.

"And how are things in the great north woods?" The Father says. He cuts through the living room, past the big coffee table. Cooper crawls out with the piece in his hand. The tassel of a flag. "So there you are, Cooper." The Father sets his suitcase down on the hearth. "Has it been raining the whole time?"

Cooper cannot answer. Cannot breathe. The shattered puzzle is his responsibility. He must put it together. Make it perfect. He cannot let anyone down. Especially The Father.

"The sun's coming out, see?" Caddie says.

Cooper does not look up. His fingers comb through the box, searching and searching for more red and white pieces.

Their mother calls from the pantry, "I thought you couldn't come this weekend."

"Don't tell me I drove all this way to be told I'm not welcome." The Father sits down in the big leather chair by the fireplace. Grandpa's chair.

The chair wheezes.

Cooper listens for mad in The Father's voice.

The Father loosens his tie.

Cooper gasps for air.

He cannot find the right red pieces for the flag of Japan. Knows they are in the box. He recognizes the gold filigree of Costa Rica's coat of arms. A bit of light blue. Maybe the ocean field of Fiji.

"I just mean I didn't expect you, or I would have planned better." Cooper's mother's voice sounds small and breakable. "Something besides spaghetti." She steps into the living room, dish towel in hand. Stops. "That's my dad's chair."

"I know it's your dad's chair."

Mad is there. Loud and clear.

"I won't hurt it," The Father says.

Piled puzzle pieces topple like tall buildings in an earthquake. The coffee table is covered with debris. That Boy must excavate. Find the survivors. He lines up the pieces. Sorts them by greens. By blues. By yellows and golds.

"Is spaghetti okay?" Cooper hears his mother ask in her small voice.

"None for me, thanks," The Father says. "I'll just relax with a glass of wine. Save my appetite for a big breakfast before Cooper and I go fishing tomorrow morning. Just the two of us."

The Father's voice, like the chirps of a singing bird, sounds happy. But Cooper knows The Father is not happy. The Father's call is a warning. *That Boy better not come with us.*

Now reds appear. Only reds. The puzzle piece pile has started to bleed.

"Whaddya say, Coop? Mom says you're a lot better up here."

The puzzle pieces blur to nothingness. Cooper feels the sudden tug on the end of his line. Watches his fishing rod bow toward the water. Hears his grandfather's voice. "You've got one! Now reel it in, my boy. Nice and steady."

Cooper reels. Reels and reels. "It's a big one," Grandpa says, pipe smoke swirling around his head in the cool morning air. "Pull it in! Pull it in!"

Grandpa is right. The fish is a big one. Cooper's arms tremble. Grandpa reaches for the rod. Pulls with all his might.

The rod snaps.

The fish gets away.

And Grandpa . . .

Grandpa falls.

As if he has pushed a replay button, Cooper sees everything all over again. Grandpa grabs an oar. When it slips through his fingers, he grabs the side of the boat. His pipe falls from his mouth. Embers fall from the pipe and roll down his shirt. Cooper scoops water from the lake. Splashes it on Grandpa's burning shirt. He stands up. The boat tips.

Cooper watches everything in the movie in slow motion—the ambulance and the flashing lights. The paramedics. The oxygen mask. The last beat of his grandfather's heart.

His mother's hands at her face.

Caddie crying.

Himself, shivering, cold and wet in the morning light.

Red, red, red. All Cooper sees is red. Blood-red. Red stripes. Red lights. Red eyes. *There was nothing you could do. Nothing you could do. Nothing you could do.* He stacks the puzzle pieces by shades and hues and tones of red.

"Maybe we could get ice cream instead," Cooper says with jitter in his voice.

"Ice cream?" The Father snorts. "You can get ice cream at home."

"But we aren't at home," Cooper says.

"Jesus Christ," The Father says. He stands up. Takes his suitcase into the bedroom beyond the kitchen.

Cooper stares at the outline of the puzzle. A hollow shell. He imagines glass walls around him like a glass moat. Soundproof walls. He can watch the world, but nothing can get in. Not even words. He imagines That Boy outside the walls. Unable to reach him. But Cooper knows That Boy watches his every move. That Boy makes sure Cooper does his job.

The spaghetti is boiled and served. The Father guesses he is hungry after all. Caddie and his mother and The Father eat without him.

Cooper picks through Pacific blue puzzle pieces, one at a time. And listens. He listens to them eating. Listens to them not talking. Knows no one is smiling. The dishes are washed and dried and put away.

"Ellen," The Father says with more mad in his voice than a swatted mud wasp.

"Not now," his mother says.

A door slams.

The cabin is silent.

Cooper turns the page of his notebook. Writes,

Silence does not feel like a safe place.

Cooper is hungry. And tired. He wishes Caddie would help him with the puzzle. Wishes they could do it together the way they used to. Like old times. South America is almost done.

"Cooper."

Cooper, Cooper, Cooper. His name bounces like bubbles against the icy glass walls. He shivers. Finds a puzzle piece. Snaps it in place. There. Chile is perfect.

"Cooper!" A whispered shout.

The bubble pops. He waits. Listens. Looks up. The cabin is dark and still except for one lamp. Like an apparition, Caddie stands in the lamp's yellow glow. "It's late. You have to go to bed. If Dad finds out you're still awake, he'll blow up."

Cooper wants to laugh at this play on words, but he cannot. He has read all about spontaneous combustion. It is not a silly idea. He cannot laugh. The Father blowing up. The Father in a million pieces. He will never laugh because he keeps his laughter a prisoner in a cage. In a deep, dark dungeon. "No, he won't," he tells Caddie so she won't be afraid. "People can't blow up. Not really."

But maybe The Father can.

"You know what I mean, Cooper." Caddie picks up an old newspaper by the fireplace, opens it wide, and lays it across the puzzle. "There," she says. "The whole world is going to sleep now."

"What time is it?" Cooper asks.

"Like, one o'clock in the morning."

"Then it's dawn in Latvia. The Balticians are waking up."

"Oh, Cooper," Caddie says. "There's no such word as Baltician."

Caddie says his name with a long "ooo" as if she is dying. He does not want her to die. He does not want The Father to blow up. He stands. He is stiff like Grandpa. His back burns under his shoulder. Fire burns in his muscles. He picks up *Inferno* and carries it to his room. Puts on his pajamas. Spots Amicus in his water dish—his head above the surface. Amicus is hungry. Cooper's heart sinks. Even though that is just a saying, he is sure he is stepping on his own heart.

"Amicus," he whispers, "I'm sorry. I almost forgot." He gives him a food nugget and pats the frog's head very gently.

With the stealth of a nocturnal animal, his flashlight in his hand, Cooper tiptoes outside, barefoot, across pine needles and acorns, to the outhouse, and then back to the kitchen. He pumps the pump slowly, quietly. He washes his hands and his face. Brushes his teeth. He hears whispers behind the walls and then silence behind the stream of pump water. When he holds the pump handle steady, he hears the word "sick."

The Father is sick to death. Sick and tired. Suddenly, the words are not whispers. "He was better," his mother says, and Cooper can picture her dark and desperate eyes. "Today we played a game, just like we used to. He was fine until . . ."

She does not finish her sentence. No one talks. Cooper feels the cold of the unsaid words. He feels the cold of his mother's thoughts. Senses the cold of The Father's icy glare. Shivers. And listens. With all his might.

"Until I got here," The Father says.

"I think you scare him."

"Well, he scares me."

"But you're the grown-up." His mother pauses. "Help him."

"And do what? Just let him act like this? If you think that's okay, then you're as crazy as he is."

"His new doctor says we're not supposed to get mad. We're supposed to let Cooper decide when—"

"His new doctor is an ignoramus. Just like the rest of them."

"He's a renowned expert and we're lucky to have him. What do you expect anyway? An overnight miracle? He's a little boy. What do you want from him?"

"I . . . I . . ."

What? What does The Father want? Cooper cannot hear him. He leans his ear to the door.

"I want my son back. Is that too much to ask?"

Silence.

Breaths.

A hand on the bedroom doorknob.

"I just want everything to go back to normal."

Normal, normal, normal. Normal is in a cage with being good. With his laughter. With his real smiles. Cooper wants to let normal go free but he can't. Or everyone will die.

"And what if that never happens?" his mother says. "Then what?"

Then what?

Cooper doesn't know the answer. Doesn't want to know the answer. Toothpaste bubbles in his mouth. Runs down his chin. He grabs a paper napkin. Rips it in half.

"You can't blame him for everything," his mother says.

Cooper wads up the pieces of napkin and pushes them into his ears. He knows he looks silly, like a billy goat.

A door creaks. Cooper hurries. The Father

bumps into Cooper in the kitchen.

"Jesus Christ," The Father says, shaking his head with eyes that might laugh and a mouth that could cry. Cooper knows The Father sees That Boy. Only That Boy. Even when That Boy is hiding, scared to death, deep inside him. Cowering next to his secrets.

Cooper steps back, lets The Father pass because he is dressed and carrying his suitcase and he is the one in a hurry.

The screen door squeaks open and snaps shut.

The dark car grumbles away through the dark woods.

Cooper must read. Read so The Father will not swerve off the highway and have a car accident and burst into flames. Read so his mother will not die of loneliness.

He crawls into bed with his flashlight.

A. A. A. Beast. Beast. Beast. Fled. Fled. Fled. Down. Down. Down . . . A beast fled down the valley with a hiss. A beast fled down the valley . . .

The cabin feels quiet. A scary kind of quiet.

Cooper yanks the wadded-up paper napkin from one ear. Still he hears nothing. Knows he hears sadness. He hears its heaving, sighing breaths. Empty human air. Nothingness blares in his ears. He hears

Amicus not croaking. His mother's hope sucked out and gone. *His mother's hope!* What day is it? Cooper shines his flashlight at his calendar. At the circle and the X and the big red arrow.

He has almost forgotten.

In the kitchen, he raises the pump handle slowly, steadily. Up and down without a screech. He fills the antique cream pitcher with water and trickles it on the ivy. The dead ivy, but there is nothing you can do about that now. *Not your fault. Not your fault. Not your fault.*

But it is.

Cooper crawls back into bed with his flashlight, his dictionary, a pencil, and his notebook. He opens the dictionary to the word *fault*. "A crack in the Earth's surface. A failure. A wrongdoing." So he never forgets, he writes this down:

Do not crack. Do not stop. Do not fail. Ever.
Or someone you love will die. And it will be
all your fault.

COINCIDENCES

The big black ant runs along the straight line where the kitchen cabinet meets the wood floor. Like a race car in its track. The ant carries a crumb the size of its head. A speck of burned toast, as far as Cooper can tell. Cooper writes in his notebook:

> The strength of small things should never be underestimated.

Cooper is careful not to step on the ant. He would never hurt a fly. But he could. By accident.

The ant escapes the shadow of the giant human and disappears into the slit between the wall and the floor. With hundreds of other ants. Thousands. Millions. Billions.

Seething with countless bugs.

An infinity of insects.

No. No. No.

Cooper puts his magnifying glass, notebook, and pencil on the kitchen counter. Try a happy thought. Just one happy thought. Like this: *Today will be a good day. Today will be a good day. Today will be a good day.*

Cooper takes a big breath. He has thought a very big thought.

A very heavy, big thought.

He takes another big breath and gets ready for another big thought.

Today he will be the master controller of his thoughts. He is a thinker. He will think other thoughts. And he will make a promise.

Today I will not scare anyone away.

Not even an ant.

Cooper lifts the pump handle. Water streams. He brushes his teeth, up and down. He wants to count, doesn't want to count. Must not count. *No counting. No counting. No counting.* He closes his eyes and spits in the sink. One, two, three times. He can't help counting. He pumps the white foam he cannot see down the drain, where it seeps into the earth around the helpless worms.

Don't think about the worms. Don't think about the worms. Don't think about the worms. He opens his eyes. Thinks about the white foam. The frothy white foam hanging in the drain like sticky, melted marshmallows.

His mother comes home from doing the laundry and running errands. Cooper runs outside. "Hi, Mom."

"Good morning, Cooper. You're up earlier than I expected." She drags a heavy basket of clean clothes from the back of the van. "I thought I'd hang everything on the line. Save a little money this time." She sets the basket in the yard. "Can you help me bring in the groceries?"

Cooper carries a bag of groceries. And then another. And then another. One, two, three. Three is perfect. *No counting. No counting. No counting.* He thinks a happy thought. He thinks of melted marshmallows and chocolate bars and graham crackers. "Did you get the s'more stuff?"

"I did, but I forgot the ice cream. I'm sorry."

Ice cream. Cooper has missed his favorite food the way he misses Grandpa. He feels his own sadness creeping inside him, growing outward from the center of his heart. He is hungry for his grandfather. Hungry for ice cream. *Hungry, hungry, hungry.* Except he doesn't know how he can be hungry for anything when he has stuffed himself full of worry and secrets. "That's okay," he says. He does not want his mother to be sorry.

But it is not okay. Nothing is okay. The Father has gone home. His mother is sad. And it's all Cooper's fault. He is only pretending everything is okay. And so is his mother.

Sometimes you can't tell the truth or it will hurt someone's feelings.

His mother folds a grocery bag. "There's a garage sale up the road," she says. "The Bells' place." She stands on her tiptoes to put away the cereal. Cooper helps. He rearranges the spices to make room for the bag of marshmallows. "I thought you and Caddie might like to take a look."

"Go where?" Caddie says. She yawns in the kitchen doorway in her polar bear pajamas.

"A garage sale," Cooper says. "But we already have one."

His mother turns around, looks at Cooper. Caddie stares too. Surprise is on their faces as if he has sneezed on them or thrown up on the floor. "That's funny, Coop," Caddie says.

Cooper imagines Caddie's words one letter at a time because they come out of her mouth so slowly. Then the words seem to surprise Caddie, as if they have all bumped into each other, and she laughs. Knowing he has made her laugh is a happy thought. The happiest thought he has had in a long time. And he knows that everything Caddie says is becoming more and more believable every day, so he believes her.

"Can we buy something?" Cooper asks.

His mother grabs her purse and opens it as fast as she can, as if her life depends on it. She pulls out two five-dollar bills. "Here, one for each of you. Go. The white house with green shutters. Just around the bend."

Caddie goes into her room and comes out wearing her bathing suit and a cover-up and sandals. Cooper follows her down the path, through the woods, and up to the sunny road. The road where the cars zoom by at fifty miles per hour. Cars that could hit you and you'd be dead. Splat. Nothing you can do about it. "Caddie, we have to walk against the traffic. Single file."

"Okay, Coop."

Caddie crosses the road. Cooper follows.

Walk, walk, walk. Listen, listen, listen. Cooper listens for cars. *Don't think about cars. Don't think about cars. Don't think about cars.* What about bears? *Bears come out at night. Bears come out at night. Bears come out at night.* Unless they are hungry. *Don't think about bears. Don't think about bears. Don't think about bears.*

Cooper wonders if he could buy a happy thought at the garage sale.

"What do you want to buy, Caddie?"

"I don't know. I might not want to buy anything."

"How will we carry it home?"

"Carry what home?

"Whatever we buy. What if it's too big to carry home?"

"Cooper!"

"What?"

"Why would you worry about carrying home something we haven't even bought yet?"

"It's important to plan ahead."

A truck engine shifts gears in the distance. A big blue truck rounds the curve, barreling up the road.

Cooper runs to catch up to Caddie. He must protect her at all costs. He grabs her arm and pulls her into the tall weeds by the side of the road. The truck swerves as if they were standing in the middle of the road and races past them.

"Cooper, let go of my arm," Caddie says as she yanks herself free.

"That truck almost hit you."

"That truck went down the middle of the road."

"But it could have hit you. One wrong move—"

"Okay, Cooper! Geez. I'll walk in the dirt."

Cooper follows Caddie, one foot in front of the other, in a straight line, at the edge of the road where the tar crumbles into the sand that spreads into the long grass that grows over the roots of the tall trees that tower over the marsh that recedes into the lake . . . *Don't think. Don't think. Don't think.* "How much farther?"

"Mom said the Bells' place. It's just around the bend."

"The white house with green shutters," Cooper says.

Gravel crunches beneath his feet. Crunches, crunches, crunches.

Just around the bend is a sign.

GArGe SALe HeRe.

"They spelled it wrong," Cooper says.

"That doesn't matter, Cooper. You still know what it means. Not everyone is a good speller." Cooper pauses to make a note.

A garage sale is a misnomer.
A misnomer means its name is wrong.

Everything is wrong.

Tables are set in the driveway and across the grass. Ragged towels have been folded. The black chair has a broken leg. Dresser drawers are open and empty. Pillows are stacked on top of books. A toilet is under a tree. Nothing is where it belongs, and everything smells like cold dirt.

Cooper stops, but Caddie winds her way through the tables of things and things and things. A maze that leads into the shadows of the garage. *What if she loses herself in the maze? Or gets lost in the briar?* She could be lost to the world until a brave knight would find her. That could take a hundred years. Or maybe forever. *Don't think. Don't think. Don't think.*

An old brown radio with knobs and knobs and

more knobs balances on a pair of sawhorses. Cooper senses a hunger in his hands. He knows That Boy wants to touch the knobs. One by one. *Don't touch. Don't touch. Don't touch.* Cooper curls his hands into fists. Puts them in his pockets.

An old man with a grumpy, wrinkled face rocks in a green chair. A metal chair that ticks like a clock with every push and sway. The old man is decrepit and rusty like his chair.

"Hey," the old man says.

"Hi," Caddie says.

"Hey," Cooper says. The man is the oldest living thing he has ever seen in his whole life. Except that is not true. The ancient sequoia trees in California are older.

"Nice to see kids interested in old stuff," the old man says with a voice that sounds like a machine slowly grinding things into tiny pieces. "Makes it easier to let it all go." He coughs. "You know what they say?" the old man says.

Cooper shakes his head.

"One man's trash is another man's treasure." The old man coughs again.

Cooper imagines the old man's cough is a volcano bursting with hot lava. Lava that rolls across the land killing everything in front of it. He steps back. Leans against a big black bell in the yard. The bell is not for sale. The old man coughs again. Coughs and coughs. Chokes and coughs. His eyes well with tears. He wipes his lips with a rag and puts the rag in his shirt pocket.

Now Cooper imagines the old man a giant salt shaker and millions of invisible microbes leaving his mouth and sprinkling the air and the dirt and the treasures and Cooper like salt. Cooper wishes the old man would cover his mouth when he coughs. He rubs the five-dollar bill in his pocket. Wants to buy everything to make the old man happy. Knows he does not want to buy anything at all. He sneaks his notebook from his pocket.

Sometimes the smallest things cause the biggest problems.

"This is really old," Caddie says. She holds a small brown book. Turns the yellowed pages slowly. Carefully. "Wow. Listen to this. 'Dear Caddie, Roses are red, violets are blue. You're my best friend, truer than true. Alice M. June 15th, 1901.' It's an autograph book. And it belonged to someone named Caddie."

Truer than true. Truer than true. Truer than true.
Cooper steps in for a closer look.

"Caddie Fremont," the old man says. "My mother's big sister."

"That's my name too," Caddie says.

"No, it isn't. Your name is Caddie Mills Cameron," Cooper tells her.

The old man laughs. A hoarse laugh. He reaches for the rag in his pocket. Rocks in his chair. "Caddie's close enough, don't you think?" He closes his mouth. Puts the rag to his lips and swallows his gurgling cough.

"How much is it?" Caddie asks.

"You just keep it," the old man says. "It's meant to be yours."

Caddie reads another page in the little book without moving her lips.

Cooper nudges her. Whispers. "Say thank you." He does not want to upset the old man. Does not want him to open his mouth again.

"Thank you," Caddie says. "Thank you."

"Much obliged," the old man says. He waves a horsefly away from his nose. Squints in the sun. "You two any relation to Pat Mills?"

Caddie is reading the whole book. Every page.

Cooper nudges her again. "He was our grandfather," Caddie says.

"Thought so," the old man says. "He was an old friend of mine. I'm Jerry Bell."

"Nice to meet you," Caddie says. Her eyes stay on the page.

Cooper looks up. Sees Mr. Jerry Bell wink his left eye.

"Now we need something for the lad here." Mr. Jerry Bell pushes himself up from his chair. Walks as slowly as a sloth toward Cooper. As curled up as a question mark. "You like to fish?"

Cooper shakes his head. He hears a gurgle in Mr. Jerry Bell's throat and steps back, watching his mouth closely for spewing lava.

"That can't be. Every boy likes to fish."

"That is not a true statement," Cooper says. He thinks of Grandpa. Pictures his burning shirt. Sees the dead ivy on the windowsill. He wants to stomp his leg. He crinkles the five-dollar bill in his pocket. Pinches his leg to hold it still. *No. No. No.*

That Boy was not invited to the garage sale.

"Then I guess times have changed. In my day, every boy liked to fish." Mr. Jerry Bell curls his knuckles, steadies himself against the table. Reaches for a bucket with a big metal crank on top. "You like ice cream?"

"Yes," Cooper says as the sun shines through the trees, speckling light on the table and all the things for sale. "Ice cream is my favorite food."

"Mine too," Mr. Jerry Bell says with another wink. He picks up the bucket with shaking arms. Turns the crank. Blue-green veins bulge in his bony hands. "This thing here is an ice cream maker."

Cooper leans forward. Examines the bucket in Mr. Bell's arms. "How do you turn it on?"

"It works the old-fashioned way. By hand. Takes patience."

"Cooper has lots of patience," Caddie says.

Truer than true. Truer than true. Truer than true.

Mr. Jerry Bell extends his shaking arms. Gives the bucket to Cooper. "There you go, my boy. Now all you need is rock salt, ice, cream, sugar, and a flavor. You pick some of them wild blackberries across the way and you'll have the best ice cream you ever ate in your whole life."

Cooper is worried about Mr. Jerry Bell. His arms take a long time to bend. Words take a long time to leave his mouth. Every breath scratches his throat, in and out.

"Kind of heavy, though," Mr. Bell says before he coughs.

Cooper wraps his arms around the bucket. It is heavy. As heavy as Cooper's worry about Mr. Bell. "I'm strong," Cooper says. "Thank you, sir."

"You can call me Mr. Bell. No one's called me sir since the army."

"Thank you, Mr. Bell. I believe this ice cream maker was meant for me."

Mr. Bell laughs. Laughs until he coughs. Coughs until he spits on the ground.

Cooper wonders what's so funny.

"Yes, I do believe it was meant for you." Mr. Bell looks at Caddie. Finds her eyes. "You carry the crank," he says.

Caddie carries the crank in one hand and the antique autograph book in the other. "C'mon, Cooper. We better get home."

Cooper nudges Caddie again. "Thank you, Mr. Bell," she says.

Cooper hugs the ice cream maker. Turns to follow Caddie.

Wait a minute.

Mr. Bell called him "my boy." *My boy*, just like Grandpa used to say.

Cooper turns back.

Mr. Bell slowly raises his hand. It quivers in the air. The ice cream maker is too heavy to hold with one hand. Cooper cannot wave back. He nods his head.

Mr. Bell's grumpy mouth slowly turns into a smile.

Cooper can tell with one look. It's there. In his eyes.

Mr. Bell is holding on for dear life.

HEAVY THINGS

Twenty-one, plop, *twenty-two,* plop, *twenty-three,* plop . . . The branches of the blackberry bushes are stiff and prickly. They scratch at Cooper's arms and legs. The scratches burn like fire.

"Ow," Caddie says. "Ow," she says a second later, before she sucks on her fingertip. Before she stomps out of the thicket. "This is impossible."

So far Cooper has picked twenty-seven berries. Twenty-seven perfect berries. *Don't count. Don't count. Don't count. Just pick, pick, pick.* The ones that fall to the ground he leaves for the birds.

"Why can't we just go to the store and buy ice cream? These thorns are killing me."

Killing, killing, killing. Cooper stops. Eyes Caddie head to toe. She needs him. "You hold the bucket," Cooper says. "I'll fill it."

Picking, picking, picking. Patience, patience, patience.
Cooper fills the bucket with perfect blackberries and
they take turns carrying it all the way home.

"How was it?" their mother asks, hanging one
of Cooper's T-shirts on a clothesline strung between
two small pine trees.

"Disgusting," Caddie says. "Everything was old.
And disgusting."

"Did you meet Mr. Bell?" their mother asks, following them into the cabin.

"Him too," Caddie says.

Cooper hoists the bucket to the kitchen counter.

"Oh, Caddie," their mother says. "He was a
friend of my dad's, you know."

"I'm just saying he's so old he's scary."

Cooper leans against the counter. Writes in his
notebook.

Sometimes things appear to be disgusting
before you understand them. Like bugs.

"What do you have there, Coop?"

Cooper looks up. Slips his notebook into his
pocket.

His mother puts her hand on the bucket of

blackberries. "What is this contraption?"

"An ice cream maker," he says. "We're going to make the best ice cream we ever ate."

"What a coincidence," his mother says. "I used to pick blackberries with my dad when I was little." She plucks a blackberry from the bucket. Pops it in her mouth. "Yum."

"And I got this. I was afraid to touch anything else," Caddie says. She holds up the autograph book. "Look at the first page."

Cooper watches his mother slowly brush her hand across the book's cover. Slowly read the first page. Slowly smile. "Another coincidence," she says. "You should take good care of this."

"I'm going to keep it up here at the cabin. On the mantel. I think it belongs someplace old," Caddie says.

"Can we make ice cream?" Cooper asks. "All we need is rock salt. And cream and sugar."

"Now?" his mother says. "I just went to the grocery store."

"Time is of the essence," he says.

His mother smiles. Gets her purse. "I'll be back in a jiffy," she says.

But she doesn't come back in a jiffy. She is late.

Cooper watches the road from the kitchen window. Watches and watches and watches. Watches the clock. Watches the gap in the trees. Watches the red cars and the white cars and the black cars whizz by. And one yellow car. He cannot take his eyes off the window. What if his mother got lost? What if she had an accident?

Finally, his mother's gray van.

Cooper races outside. Waits until the van rolls to a stop and the door opens.

"You were gone a long time. Eighty-nine minutes."

"I know it, Cooper. I had to get gas. But the gas station was all blocked off. The lady at the grocery store told me there had been a robbery, so I had to drive all the way around the lake and go to the one in New Prairie."

"A robbery?" He opens the cabin door for her. He has never thought about a robbery. Robbers are desperate and unpredictable. Sometimes they are armed. Another close call. He will add robberies to his list of worries. This cannot happen again. Ever.

"But guess what else?" his mother says.

"What else?" Cooper says as he leans on the counter and writes in his notebook,

Sometimes the most dangerous things are the things you never think of.

His mother pulls a thin newspaper from one of the grocery bags. *The North Lakes News.* "Here's a whole calendar of things to do up here. They're having turtle races on the Fourth of July." She looks back at the newspaper. "Wow, I guess that's the week after next, isn't it? Remember how much fun those used to be? Maybe you and Caddie can go."

"Turtle races are an oxymoron," Cooper says, slipping his notebook back into his pocket.

"That's why they're so much fun," his mother says, patting him on the shoulder.

She unpacks the ice cream supplies. "Let's get to work. Cooper, you can be the official crank turner. The lady in the check-out explained the whole process. She said she makes ice cream for her grandchildren all the time."

His mother rinses the blackberries. Pats them dry. She pours cream and sugar and berries into the metal container. Cooper scoops the ice. "Right there," his mother says, and Cooper carefully fills the gap between the metal container and the wooden bucket with ice and rock salt.

Caddie comes into the kitchen. Pours herself a bowl of cold cereal and reads *The North Lakes News* while she watches.

"Now it's up to you," his mother tells him.

Turn, turn, turn. Wait, wait, wait. Turn, turn, turn.

"Oh, boy," Caddie says. "Turtle races on the Fourth of July."

"You can take Cooper," their mother says.

"I can't wait," Caddie says. She slurps the milk in her bowl. "How long does this ice-cream-making business take?" She sets her empty bowl in the sink. Leaves the kitchen, already bored silly. "I'm going to the beach."

Turn, turn . . .

"Maybe Dad'll go swimming with me."

Stop.

"Dad's not here," their mother calls to Caddie. She doesn't look up. Not even when Caddie comes back in the kitchen with a frown on her face. She is too busy adding more rock salt to the bucket to look up. "He had to go back home."

Caddie slumps against the doorframe. "But he just got here."

"He forgot about something at work."

"Why didn't he say goodbye?"

Cooper knows why The Father left. Knows why The Father didn't say goodbye. Knows it has nothing to do with work. He pushes on the crank. It barely moves.

"He left really early. I'm sure he didn't want to wake you."

"It was still dark out," Cooper says.

It *was* still dark out. Cooper isn't lying. But he is lying.

Sometimes keeping the truth a secret is the same thing as telling a lie.

His heart feels heavy. As heavy as the bucket of blackberries.

Now his mother looks at him. Worried. "Did you hear him? Did he wake you up?"

Cooper shakes his head. He knows he's telling another lie while he tries his best to tell the truth. "I heard his car."

His mother's eyes rest on his face for a long time. He can see his mother wonder if Cooper heard them talking. He can see her sadness. He can see her hide her secrets, and he wonders if she can see him hide his.

"I can't turn the crank anymore. It's stuck," he says.

89

"That just means it's done," his mother says, suddenly smiling.

Cooper lifts up the crank. Removes the cover of the bucket, and he and his mother peer into the ice cream maker like they're looking into a deep hole, trying to see the bottom. And there it is. Ice cream. Real ice cream. Like magic. Thick yellow-white ice cream with dark streaks and chunks of blackberries.

"Look at that," his mother says.

"Look at that," Cooper says. And he wishes Caddie and his mother liked ice cream as much as he does so they could forget that The Father drove away in the darkest part of the morning without saying goodbye. Not even to their mother.

Caddie looks into the bucket too. "Wow," she says.

Cooper sticks his finger in the ice cream like a hook and puts a glob in his mouth. Swirls it with his tongue and swallows. "Mr. Bell was right. This is the best ice cream I've ever eaten in my whole life."

Caddie gets three spoons from the drawer, hands them out like tickets. Their mother scoops the ice cream into bowls, and they stand at the kitchen counter and eat ice cream. Bite after bite. They eat the blackberry ice cream until it is all gone.

"I can't believe we did that," Caddie says, scraping

her spoon against the empty metal bucket. "If Dad were here, he'd be mad."

Nobody says anything.

Their mother doesn't even say, "Now, Caddie."

Cooper looks away. Looks at the clock. The *tick, tick, tick* of the second hand is the only sound.

Maybe his mother finally sees that everything Caddie says is getting more and more believable every day.

Eleven seconds is an eternity in the silence.

A silence too heavy for the muscles in Cooper's brain.

Twelve, thirteen. "Let's play Monopoly," Cooper says.

"Finally, something *I* want to do," Caddie says.

"That would be fun," says their mother.

"I'll be the banker," says Cooper.

He runs to the armoire. Looks up. Spots Monopoly between the Scrabble game and the stack of jigsaw puzzles. *Birds of the World* catches his eye. He pictures the free-falling spill of *Flags of the World.* Knows the finished flag puzzle sits on the coffee table behind him. Perfect and untouched. *No, no, no.* He does not want to go anywhere near the armoire.

"Caddie, can you get it?"

"What am I, your personal maid?"

Caddie rolls her eyes and sighs all at once. She sets the game on the dining room table. Before Cooper sits down, she has grabbed the colorful stack of Monopoly money. "I'll organize it, Coop," she says. "Otherwise, we'll be here forever. You can still be the banker."

Caddie lays the money in neat piles in front of Cooper. Rolls the die. *No, not die—dice. Dice. Dice. Dice.* Even if it is only one.

When they take a break for dinner, Cooper owns Park Place and twelve hotels. He lines up his money by color.

"Now it's time for s'more ice cream," he says. "Get it?"

"You're crazy," Caddie says.

"I know," Cooper says.

"I didn't mean it like that," Caddie says.

"I know," Cooper says again.

Caddie puts her hand on Cooper's head. Musses his hair. "I get to crank it this time," Caddie says.

Cooper breaks up the graham crackers. His mother cuts up the sticky marshmallows. Cooper stacks the squares of the chocolate bar in a perfect chocolate tower.

Caddie cranks the ice cream for one minute and eighteen seconds. "This is boring," she says. She keeps cranking, for four minutes and twenty-seven seconds. "I can't take this anymore."

"I can," Cooper says. He cranks and cranks the ice cream. Switches hands and cranks and cranks and cranks. Switches hands again. He cranks and cranks until the crank can't budge another millimeter. "I think it's done," he says.

They decide to eat s'more ice cream first, and then they have tuna fish sandwiches for dessert. Cooper is surprised. Dinner is out of order. He feels uneasy, but That Boy must not be paying attention.

"I can't eat another bite," Caddie says.

"Me either," their mother says.

"I can," Cooper says.

"Let's finish the game," Caddie says.

They play Monopoly into the night. Their mother goes bankrupt and picks up her knitting. "I think I'll call it a day."

Caddie passes Go. Cooper counts out the money. Face up. He matches the colors and the edges. "One, two, three . . ."

"Cooper," Caddie says. "Don't."

Cooper counts as fast as he can.

Caddie wins and it's time for bed.

Cooper holds out his hand to Caddie. She takes his hand in hers. Reluctantly. Raises an eyebrow. "It was an honor to do business with you today," he says, bowing.

"Good night, Cooper," Caddie says.

Cooper goes into his room and looks at his calendar. He puts a checkmark on today. Sixty-seven days to go. Sixty-seven days to think happy thoughts. Only sixty-seven long days. He gives Amicus a food nugget. Amicus the Great is a happy thought. "You're a good, brave boy and I love you."

He reaches for his toes and sends the sand to the floor and then he flops backward on his bed. His right arm aches from cranking the crank. His stomach hurts. He is too tired to read. Too tired to write in his notebook. But he knows he is not as tired as old Mr. Bell.

Caddie's footsteps creak in the hallway.

"Caddie?" he calls.

She stops. Opens his bedroom door. Peeks her head in. "What?"

"Let's take him some ice cream."

"Who?"

"Mr. Bell."

"I guess," she says. "We'll have to make more. You ate it all."

"That's okay. My arm hurts, but I'm up to it."

Caddie sniffs. Wrinkles her nose and sniffs again. "You know your room stinks." She walks up to Amicus. Eye-to-eye. "I think it's time to clean his aquarium."

"You hurt his feelings," Cooper says.

"That's not possible. He's a reptile."

"He's an amphibian."

"So he's an amphibian, then. He still doesn't have any feelings."

"How do you know? His heart is bigger than ours."

"No, it isn't."

"We only have two chambers. He has three." Cooper watches Caddie tap on the glass. "Tell him you're sorry," he says. "And give him a food nugget. He deserves it."

Caddie rolls her eyes. Opens the food jar. "I'm sorry," she says to the glass. She lifts the screen cover, drops a food nugget on Amicus's head. "There you go, Amicus."

"You mean, Amicus the Great."

"Since when?"

"Since he proved his bravery in the midst of battle."

Caddie stares at Amicus. Smiles without rolling her eyes. Sighs gently. "You know what, Coop?"

"What?"

"You hardly did anything weird all day."

Cooper feels his heart shiver. It feels like his birthday. But it is not his birthday. And he cannot pretend it is. Cannot pretend it is easy to not do anything weird.

Caddie can't see where he has stuffed his thoughts and his worries. But Cooper knows where they are. Always knows where they are. He feels his secrets in his pockets, between his toes, crammed inside his head. Filling up the empty spaces between his ideas and his words. Happy thoughts are hard. Exhausting. Mind-boggling. Happy thoughts are harder than counting and touching and reading three times three.

"Really?" he asks.

"Really."

Cooper smiles. A true smile. He smiles because he cannot stop the smile. He is too exhausted to stop the smile. He smiles because everything Caddie says is getting more and more believable every day. He swears he can feel his cheeks lift into the air.

Today he is weak enough to let himself smile.

COMPETITIONS

"Where did you get your turtle?" Caddie asks a lady in orange shorts and giant sunglasses holding a mud turtle with just the fingertips of both hands.

"Over there," the lady says, but Cooper doesn't look in the direction she points. He's watching the kids find their places around the circle, the big green circle painted in the center of the parking lot of DJ's Liquors. In the center of the circle is a painting of a mud turtle and the word "WINNER." The paint is wearing off, but Cooper knows what it says.

If you don't bring your own turtle, you must rent one for five dollars, and if you don't keep it, or step on it, then you get half your money back. *Kinosteridae* are omnivorous and will eat a small tadpole or frog. As long as Amicus is a living thing, Cooper knows he will not keep a mud turtle as a pet. And he will be very careful not to step on one.

A little girl with pigtails and purple balls the size of suckers in her hair hugs her turtle. He is injured. His shell is chipped. She kisses its pointed green nose. Holds it up to her father. "Don't be scared, Daddy. He's supposed to be ugly." Her father pulls a clump of tissues from his pocket. Wipes the little girl's mouth. Wipes his hands.

Cooper circles the crowd. Crouches by bare knees and strollers. When the whistle blows, turtle holders let go. Bales and bales of turtles crawl in different directions. They leave trickles of water in their paths. People shout and laugh and point. Cooper now understands the meaning of *cacophony*. He thinks of gym class. Thinks of dodgeball. He remembers the gym teacher pointing at the sidelines with a long waggling finger and a mad face. Cooper knows the turtles are embarrassed. Ashamed. They don't know what to do. They don't know the rules. He covers his ears.

A turtle crawls across the green edge of the circle, the wrong way. It crawls fast, through everyone's legs, and bumps into Cooper's tennis shoe. Its shell is chipped. Cooper picks up the turtle with both hands and holds it close to his chest. "You're not ugly," he says.

Long, hairy legs in shorts stride toward Cooper. He looks up.

"That's not yours," says the man with the clump of tissues still clenched in his hand.

"I know," Cooper says. "He's lost."

"He is not lost," the man says. "He belongs to my daughter."

The little girl reaches for the turtle. Cries. "That's mine."

Cooper hugs the turtle. Whispers, "I'm sorry." He puts the turtle on the ground. Backs up, out of the crowd, past the angled yellow lines of the parking lot, and sits on the curb. Sits far away from the painted circle. And pulls out his notebook.

Making fun of something is different from having fun.

"Cooper!" Caddie's mad voice shouts. "I've been looking all over for you." Caddie grabs his arm. "You have to rent a turtle."

"I don't want to."

"You have to," Caddie says. "Mom said. And here's five dollars." Caddie holds out five one-dollar bills.

"Here *are*," he says.

"Geez, Cooper." Caddie shakes her head. "And you have to hurry. Mom will be back for us soon. You already missed the first race."

Cooper shakes his head too. He didn't miss the first race. He saw the injured turtle get lost and crawl in the wrong direction. He does not want to be here. Does not want to feel embarrassed for the turtles.

"You have to," Caddie says. She shoves the money into his hand. The bills are brand new. Crisp and sharp. He wants to count them. Wants to touch the four pointed corners . . .

"Don't worry, Coop. I already put it in order for you."

He fans the edges of the bills. She did it right. She is a good sister. "Let's buy ice cream, okay?"

"No, Cooper. You've had enough ice cream to last a lifetime. C'mon."

"Let's go on the Whirly Bird."

"Rides make me sick. You know that. Besides, this'll be fun for you. But they're almost out of turtles."

Caddie pulls Cooper all the way to the picnic area, under a big white tent. Plastic ice cream buckets cover the ground. Kicked on their sides. Upside down. The grass is stomped on, bright green and muddy. "The guy said he'd save you one. His name is Todd and he's really nice. And cute."

Cooper does not care about cute, but that word, *Todd*, sounds sharp. Urgent. And something else. Cooper must pay attention.

Only two turtles remain in the last bucket, scraping their claws against the plastic prison, crawling over each other like the lobsters in the tank at the grocery store at home. Cooper imagines the tank tipped over, spilling water and lobsters across the floor. Lobsters crawling their way to freedom.

"That your little brother?" asks the voice. A boy voice. A voice Cooper remembers. A voice that burns across his skin like a smoking match.

"Yeah," Caddie says. "This is Cooper. He's a little shy at first. Cooper? Cooper, turn around."

Cooper does not turn around.

"Here's the one I saved for him."

That voice again. Cooper is certain of it. The voice goes with a tan and cut-off shorts. And a grin that never stops.

"Be polite, Cooper." Caddie pulls on Cooper's shoulder. He shifts a little. Looks up. Looks straight into the eyes of The Grinner. The Grinner holds out a flailing green turtle. "He's a fast one," The Grinner says, grinning. "I guarantee it."

Cooper looks down at the muddy grass. Puts his foot in someone else's footprint. Someone bigger, stronger. Brave.

"Cooper!" Caddie says with more mad in her voice than noise. "You say thank you, Cooper. Right now."

Cooper can't say thank you. He can't speak at all. He turns away. Hurries to a picnic table outside the tent and sits down. He turns his back, but he can still feel Caddie talking to The Grinner. He feels her anger beneath her smile. Anger for him, a smile for The Grinner. From the corner of his eye, Cooper can see Caddie bounce like a puppy as she turns away from The Grinner.

"Hey, Caddie," The Grinner yells after her. "See you tonight. The one with the red mailbox. Mills, right?"

"Yup!" Caddie calls back. "Seven-thirty sharp."

"Don't forget!"

Cooper turns his head toward Caddie. He feels his stomach turn upside down. Feels his world turn from east to west.

Some forces in the world are too powerful to
be stopped.

"I won't forget," Caddie shouts over her shoulder,
smiling a smile as big as the ones the models smile in
her magazines. She is moving in slow motion, smiling, with red lipstick on her lips and the wind blowing back her blond hair. With the slightest tilt of her
head she could lift off and fly away.

But where will Caddie land?

What if he isn't there in time?

What if he cannot catch her?

Cooper can feel The Grinner's grin creep all
the way across the muddy grass. And someone else
tiptoeing up behind him. Someone worried and
frustrated. It's That Boy. That Boy knows: The
Grinner is not to be trusted. And now Cooper can't
stop himself.

He rubs his hands as if he is washing them. Rubs
and scrubs as if water is pouring forth from the pump
and it is safe and clean and everlasting. He holds his
arms over his head and washes them in the air.

In the blur and splash, Cooper spies Tall Boy
carrying buckets. Buckets and buckets. He hears
the scratching of tiny claws on plastic. Desperate

claws. He hears Tall Boy call, "Hey, Todd. I've got five more." Tall Boy's head turns. His eyes target Cooper, then Caddie, then Cooper again. Cooper scrubs harder and harder. Reaches higher and higher. He stands. Looks up. Maybe the sun will dry his hands.

"Don't, Cooper. Please stop. Everyone is watching. Please. Todd will see you too. Please stop. You're embarrassing me."

Stop it now before you embarrass yourself. The Father's words pound in his head. *Pound. Pound. Pound.* But Cooper does not care about embarrassing himself. Only cares about Caddie. He must save her. He must, must, must save Caddie from The Grinner.

Caddie holds out the turtle. "Take the turtle, Cooper."

Caddie's face is red. Beet-red. Flag-red. Blood-red.

Turtle water drips on Cooper's foot. Turtle legs wave in the air. He must save the turtle too.

"Please." Caddie is desperate.

The turtle is desperate.

Cooper grabs the wet turtle from Caddie, runs across the parking lot. Carries the turtle like a football. He runs across the train tracks. Runs across the road. Hears the car's brakes before he feels the blaring horn vibrate in his chest.

"Cooper, stop!"

He keeps running. Past the gas station. Past the playground. Into the woods. He runs and runs. Runs to save the turtle. Hears Caddie running behind him.

"Cooper, please stop!"

Caddie stops. She needs to catch her breath.

Cooper keeps running. Runs to put the turtle in the reeds by the edge of the lake. Runs to save all the turtles that do not know why they are in the hot sun, watched and laughed at and yelled at by strangers, when all they want to do is be left alone to find their way home safe and sound.

They don't understand.

No one understands.

"Touchdown!" Cooper yells from the edge of the lake. He wants Caddie to laugh.

Caddie catches up to him. "What is wrong with you?" She shouts. "That car almost hit you!"

Wrong. Wrong. Wrong. Everything is wrong. Too much is wrong. So wrong Cooper does not know where it will end. Does not know where to begin. Happy thoughts are impossible.

Cooper sits down and pulls out his notebook. Writes, breathlessly,

Sometimes right is wrong and wrong is right.

Caddie pulls Cooper to his feet. To the edge of the road. She watches the traffic. Waits for the big giant motorhome to go by before she pulls him to the parking lot. To their mother's van parked in front of the Pizza Pie and I pizza parlor.

"Right on time," their mother says. "How was everything?"

"Great," Caddie says. "Just great." She gets in the van. Slams the door. Rolls down her window and leans on her elbow.

The van picks up speed on the main road.

Caddie watches the trees go by.

Cooper watches the trees go by.

Trees that blur to nothingness.

His mother glances in the rearview mirror. "Cooper? How about you?"

"Great," he says.

Caddie says "great" because she is mad. And because she doesn't want to talk about it.

Cooper says "great" because he is scared. There is

so much to worry about. And time is of the essence. But no one understands.

He is scared for the turtles. The not-ugly turtles that look just the way they are supposed to look. They know they are in danger and they want to be safe. If they are safe, no one can see them. If no one can see them, no one will know what they look like. No one will call them ugly.

Mostly, Cooper is scared for Caddie.

He opens his notebook.

Humans do not have tough shells. They do not have camouflage.

They stand out where they don't belong.

Caddie does not know she is in danger.

The wind is still in her hair.

EAVESDROPPING

Cooper sits on the sofa reading. His never-ending book, *Inferno* by Dante, is getting heavier. Heavier than a bucket of sand. Heavier than the ice cream maker full of blackberries and rock salt. Too heavy to read. Cooper reads one more sentence. The sentence about the "just man," whose face is outwardly kind.

Kind, kind, kind. Cooper thinks of Mr. Bell. His old face is grumpy, but his eyes are kind. He puts his finger on the comma. *Comma, comma, comma.*

Caddie's bedroom door opens. She walks through the living room. Scowls at Cooper. Then she goes into their mother's room and shuts the door.

A mystery. A secret. Cooper needs to know what is so mysterious.

He closes the book on Canto XVII. Tiptoes to his mother's closed door.

"No, Mom, he's getting worse. You should have seen him. I've never seen him do that before—like he was washing his hands in the air. But there wasn't any water."

Cooper strains to hear what his mother says. Cannot hear a word. He pictures his mother in her closet, putting away clothes. He watches a big black ant crawl from a crack in the wooden floor. Caddie pauses, talks. Talks as if she is talking to herself. "It was worse than ever."

A whisper. His mother?

The black ant crawls along the baseboard. Slips into another crack.

Cooper puts his ear to the door.

"I am not being selfish," Caddie says. "I play with him. I took him to the turtle races just like you wanted. But if he embarrasses me one more time, I'm not going to do it anymore. He needs help."

His mother's soft steps approach the door. "You know we've tried everything."

"But, Mom, you can't give up."

His mother's footsteps recede. "I'm not the one giving up."

Caddie sighs. "Maybe he needs to go someplace."

Cooper can't bear to listen. But he cannot move.

No, he thinks. *No, no, no. I'll be good. I won't count. I won't. I won't. I won't.* But how will he protect them? They don't understand. They don't understand how good he already is. How careful he has to be for them.

He remembers chewing without counting. He remembers reading words and sentences and pages once and only once. He remembers being happy. He remembers having friends. He would like to have a friend again.

I can be good again. I know, I know, I know I can.

Cooper will try. Try harder than ever. He will try with all his might not to count, not to touch, not to wash. He will try to find more happy thoughts and make them stick in his mind.

He does not want to go someplace.

Ever.

Cooper sneaks across the cabin, into his room. He retrieves the magnifying glass, a pencil, and his notebook and returns to the closed door.

"Now you sound like your father. Like he's some kind of freak. Do you want to think of your little brother as some kind of freak?"

A freak is a mutation. A glitch in hereditary material.

A mutant. A subspecies. People are not subspecies.

Cooper is not a freak. It's That Boy. If That Boy would just go away. Leave him alone.

He doesn't want to hear anything more, but he must listen to every word. His heart beats hard. Still, he will remain brave. He must pretend he has not been sliced in two by the laser-hot words.

Eavesdropping is a daring act of heroism. The listener must keep all the words to himself. Like swallowed food.

". . . can't be happy like this." Cooper hears the words sneak under the door. Who can't be happy like this? He has missed important words, but it doesn't matter. Cooper knows this one certain sadness: no one is happy. He writes these words on the next page:

Sometimes people pretend to be happy with jokes and ice cream and games.

"He's just a little boy. You know what the doctors said. He might even grow out of it. We just have to be patient."

"That's like saying a dog will turn into a cat. Maybe if you wait two million years."

"Oh, Caddie . . ."

"I mean it, Mom. I can't take it anymore. If he pulls anything tonight, I'll commit him myself."

"Where is he, by the way?"

"Where else? He's reading. In the living room."

"I think he's better up here," his mother says.

"Sometimes he's better. Like when we made ice cream. He even wanted to take some to Mr. Bell. But—"

"Poor Mr. Bell. He's in the hospital. Lung cancer. Ninety-seven years old. He knew my dad, you know."

Poor Mr. Bell. Poor Mr. Bell. Poor Mr. Bell.

"No, Mom. I mean, yes, I know he knew your dad, and I'm sorry he's sick, but that's not what we're talking about right now. We're talking about tonight."

"You said it's a barn dance?"

"They call it a barn dance, but it's in town in the old fire station by the lake."

"Where they hold the fireworks?"

"Yeah."

"Dad's coming back up this afternoon. Maybe

we can all go. I mean if he finishes his project on time. He has a lot on his mind right now."

"You're not coming to the dance, Mom. It's just for kids."

"I meant the fireworks," she says.

Another big black ant crawls out of the floorboards.

"Mom, you're not even listening to me."

"Yes, I am, but tell me again. Who's driving?"

"Mike's dad."

"And Mike is . . . ?"

"Todd's best friend. Todd is the one I'm going with. I met him at the turtle races. He lives across the lake. His dad owns the liquor store. And he's really cute. I think he likes me, but Cooper wouldn't even say thank you. God, Mom, it was so embarrassing."

"You leave Cooper to me."

Cooper does not want to watch the fireworks. What if the world cracks open? What if the ground catches on fire? But he must go. He must protect his mother and Caddie at all costs.

Footsteps cross the room. Even without his magnifying glass he can see the shadows of feet under the door. Caddie's? His mother's?

The best way to be good is to pretend you are doing something else.

Pretending is different from lying. Pretending is a different kind of truth.

Cooper picks up the magnifying glass. He holds it close to the baseboard. Monitors the crawling of another big black ant with folded wings. She must be the queen.

The queen.

Every queen needs a king. Caddie is the queen. Tonight Cooper will be her king.

When his mother's door opens, Cooper is ready to pretend. "I believe we have an infestation," he says. "Of ants."

"We're in the middle of the woods," Caddie says. "Get over it."

"Now, Caddie," his mother says and steps over Cooper's legs.

"How long have you been lying there?" Caddie asks.

"Time is a concept of spent energy," he says.

"That doesn't even make any sense. And you better get up before someone trips over you. Like me." She nudges his leg with her foot.

"Ow," he says, pretending.

"Yeah, right," Caddie says.

Pretend. Pretend. Pretend. For Caddie, Cooper must pretend his hardest. Caddie cannot be privy to the idea he hoards. The feat he must undertake. The plan to fend off The Grinner and Tall Boy begins now, with the red tablecloth in the bottom drawer in the kitchen. Cooper stands up. Straight and tall. And brave. Brave like Amicus the Great.

The rest of the afternoon, Cooper works in the garage. Grandpa's garage, filled with boards and paint and the long workbench with the anvil. The garage smells like turpentine and burnt rubber. And pipe smoke. Rakes, shovels, a pitchfork, and a hoe rust together in one corner. Cooper works hard. In silence. Just like his grandfather worked.

Sometimes it is possible to smell history.

"What are you doing?"

Cooper jumps. Drops his pencil. His mother stands in the doorway. Cooper was unprepared. Didn't hear her coming. "Making something," he says.

"What is it?" she asks, coming closer, stepping over a stack of long boards.

"A costume."

"Really?" She gives him a hug. "It's nice to see you out here. Reminds me of my dad." She smiles. "Dinner's almost ready," she says before she leaves. Then he hears the screen door squeak open and snap shut.

Tools dangle on the garage wall. He chooses the needle-nose pliers and the awl and a hammer. Finds wire and clamps. The orange hard hat will work perfectly. The whole time he bores and bends and twists, the pitchfork stands ready behind him.

He eats dinner with a secret on the tip of his tongue.

Caddie hurries to her room to get ready.

"Dad should be here any minute," his mother says, reaching for Caddie's dirty plate.

Cooper sneaks back to the garage.

Words and clanks float through the open kitchen window, past the cobwebs and dead bugs on the sill, to the depths of the garage. "I think we'll let the pots and pans soak awhile," he hears his mother say. The lake is calm, the air hot and silent. Golden sunlight crawls beneath the tree branches. The towering Norway pines stand watch, their shadows long and still.

Poised in a corner of the garage, Cooper breathes the ancient fumes of another world. The red cape and hard hat are donned. Horns bared. Pitchfork at the ready.

He waits.

And watches.

A white SUV rolls slowly down the driveway. Tall Boy drives. A man sits next to him. The Grinner's long blond hair bounces near the window in the back seat. The vehicle stops beneath the giant Norway pines.

The cabin's door squeaks open—squeaks again, louder. Cooper waits, expecting the old spring to snap. But the door slaps shut. Followed by the sound of footsteps as Cooper's mother and Caddie step across the cement stoop to the sidewalk and onto the sandy path. Caddie comes into view. She is dressed like a princess in a white sundress.

Car doors painted with leaping fish open and slam. One, a man. Two, Tall Boy. Three, The Grinner.

The man puts his left hand on Tall Boy's shoulder, holds out his right hand to Cooper's mother. "Hi. I'm Ron. Mike's dad."

"Ellen. Caddie's mom," his mother says, shaking

Ron's hand. Then she turns to Tall Boy. "You're Mike, then."

"Yeah," Tall Boy says. "Nice to meet you."

Next is The Grinner.

"So you must be Todd."

That word. *Todd.* It's urgent. Like a cue. Cooper darts forward, pitchfork first. He jumps and lands in their midst. Plants his feet in a firm stance. Horns pointed to the sky. He thrusts the pitchfork high overhead. Shouts line nine from Canto III: "Abandon all hope, you who enter here!"

The foes step back.

"Cooper!" Caddie whirls around. Her face is the color of Cooper's cape. "Mom, you promised."

But Cooper must stand his ground. He must protect Caddie at all costs.

The Grinner sneers. Turns for the car.

But Tall Boy smiles. He extends his hand toward Cooper with the chivalrous gesture of a fine gentleman. And then he wrinkles his face with worry. But Cooper can see that he is pretending. "Master," Tall Boy says, "make clear their meaning, which I find too hard to gather."

Cooper knows these words. He knows all of Dante's words in his good and famous book. He has read them three times three. He tests Tall Boy to be sure: "All fear must be left here and cowardice die."

Tall Boy stomps the ground and howls like a lonely animal. "Master, what is this I hear?"

Tall Boy has skipped parts of the good and famous book. Pages turn. The lines race through Cooper's mind until he finds the right one. "This is the powerful state of souls unsure."

"Let us not speak of them," Tall Boy says as he lowers his arms, laughs, and steps out of character. The fear recedes in Cooper like a single lapped wave. Tall Boy is clapping.

"Wow! You've read *Inferno*? Already? I can't believe it! I love that book! I had to memorize that scene for my drama class."

"And so you are well read, my fine fellow." Cooper bows.

Caddie claps her hands quickly. Smiles. She is pretending too. "I guess we better get going," she says. "Mom?"

But then Mike bows and Cooper's mother and Ron begin to clap.

The Grinner does not clap. He slugs Tall Boy in the arm. "You weirdo."

"This is Cooper," his mother says.

"Cooper must like to read as much as Mike here," Ron says.

"Nobody likes to read as much as Cooper. It's impossible," Caddie says. "Say goodbye, Cooper."

"Adieu, for now," Cooper says. "For I will remain strong and resolute."

"Mom," Caddie says.

Cooper's mother puts her hands on his shoulders. "Maybe we'll see you all up there later," she says.

But Cooper is still wary of The Grinner. And he must warn Caddie. He wriggles free from his mother's hands. "Then fare thee well, but Caddie—"

"What is it now, Cooper?" She rolls her eyes.

"Beware the bitter one." He looks at Caddie. Locks eyes with The Grinner.

The Grinner has been warned.

The car doors slam. One, two, three: Ron, The Grinner, and Caddie.

"So let your sadness be disburdened," Tall Boy says over his shoulder as he climbs into the driver's side and takes the wheel. He slams his door. Waves through the windshield.

"Do not forget, I am always at your side," Cooper calls out, then bows. His horned crown falls to the ground.

FIREWORKS

The phone rings. The clinking of pots and pans halts. "Cooper, can you get that?" his mother calls from the kitchen. "My hands are all wet."

Cooper closes his book. Walks to the old black phone on the desk. The phone with the cord. He touches its curls. One, two, three . . .

"It's probably Dad," she says.

Cooper stops. He feels the cord wrapped around him like The Father's angry words. Feels the cold in The Father's voice. Shivers. The phone rings again. Cooper cups his hands over his ears.

"Cooper?" His mother comes around the corner, drying her hands on a dish towel. The phone rings again. She picks up the receiver. "Hello," she says, and then she smiles a sad smile at the air.

Silence.

Cooper sits back down on the sofa. Reaches for his notebook.

Smiles are like costumes.

Cooper watches his mother like a tourist watching Old Faithful. Waiting for the geyser to burst. Spew. Any second now. His mother's lips almost move. She breathes. Her eyes glisten. She smiles again, this time at Cooper. "He's right here," she says. "He's growing like a weed. Do you want to talk to him?" She nods a happy nod at Cooper.

Behind her, overhead, Cooper sees the box. *Birds of the World*. He imagines the box open, spewing, colored cardboard pieces falling like rain. He imagines a flood of puzzle pieces rising around him. Imagines drowning in a sea of puzzles. His arms and legs tied together. Cooper holds his breath so he will not drown. And shakes his head.

"Oh, never mind," his mother says into the phone. "No, it's okay. I know what that promotion means to you. Us."

Cooper hears the dial tone. The phone is as good as dead. Dead as a doornail. Nothing you can do about it now. He feels his mother's heart sink. Sees her smile above her sunken heart.

Sometimes you can be standing right next to someone and still be completely alone.

Cooper knows what it is like to be completely alone. To see. To hear. To talk. To breathe. To wait. To worry. In the middle of a crowd. Alone. And keep it all a secret.

"Dad can't get away," she tells him. "He has a big project and his promotion depends on it. We'll have to watch the fireworks by ourselves."

Cooper exhales his deep breath.

His mother looks out the window, toward the pink sunset on the lake. "It'll be dark soon. Why don't we get going so we aren't late?"

They are not late. They park by the old fire station. Cooper can hear the music playing inside as they walk past the brick wall toward the hill overlooking the lake. The sky is the same blue-gray color as the water.

His mother shakes out the blanket and lays it across the weeds. A blanket with brown and yellow squares. The blanket from Grandpa's fishing boat. Cooper runs his hand across the soft blanket. Squeezes it. Pulls it across his shoulder.

The crowd grows. The hill is dotted with more and more blankets and quilts and beach towels and lawn chairs. Soon the sky settles dark and close all around them like the warm fishing blanket.

Cooper lies on his back and stares at the dark sky. He sees, hears, breathes, waits, worries. Caddie is with The Grinner.

Ka-thunk. Whistle. Spew.

The first rocket shoots into the black sky. A sudden dawn. Then black again. Suddenly, sparks trickle like icy rain. Cooper watches the whole sky, certain he can see its curvature from edge to edge. He watches his mother relax and smile. True smiles as she oohs and ahhs with the crowd.

But Cooper cannot relax.

Ka-thunk, whistle, spew.

Cooper closes his eyes. Covers his ears. Caddie should be watching the fireworks with them. Not dancing with The Grinner.

Cooper's stomach is sick with worry.

He sits up and watches the big open door of the old fire station. He watches as boys and girls like Caddie spill out of the dance and move across the lawn in the shadows. Then he spots Tall Boy. In the doorway. Alone.

"The dance is over," Cooper says. "I'll go get Caddie."

"Come right back," his mother says.

Cooper steps between the blankets and chairs. "Hey, watch it," someone says.

Watch it. Watch it. Watch it.

Behind him, another rocket shoots into the sky. *Ka-thunk, whistle, spew.*

Tall Boy leans against an old green gas pump, watching the sky shatter with color. "Hi, Mike," Cooper says.

Tall Boy shifts his stance. Looks away as if Cooper is a stranger.

Cooper stands in front of him. "It's me. Cooper. I'm not wearing my horns and cape, so it's hard to recognize me."

"What?" Tall Boy frowns at him. Cooper can see him remember. "Oh, yeah. Hi."

Ka-thunk, whistle, spew.

Tall Boy looks back at the sky. "Cool," he says.

"Cool," Cooper says, looking where Tall Boy looks. "Where's Caddie?"

Tall Boy's arms are folded. He doesn't turn his

head to talk to Cooper. He talks to the sky. "She took a walk."

"A walk?" Cooper says.

"Yeah. A walk. With Todd."

Ka-thunk, whistle . . .

The rocket shakes the ground. Vibrations rise from Cooper's feet into his stomach. That word, *Todd*, burns in his gut. Just like that word, *Dad*. Worry spews from Cooper's mouth and he imagines himself a fire-breathing dragon. "WHERE?" Cooper shouts at the top of his lungs above the cacophony of music, laughter, crackles, and millions of oohs and ahhs.

Tall Boy loses his balance. Slips away from the pump. Catches himself. "Geez. Keep it down." He looks around. Whispers, "In the park."

Cooper wishes he still had his helmet and cape. And the pitchfork. "Help me find her."

"No," Tall Boy says. "They want to be alone."

Cooper imagines every nerve in his body alive, desperate, reaching out. The gravel burns hot beneath his feet. Burns through his shoes. Every last drop of water in the moat has evaporated. He pulls on Tall Boy's arm. "Help me find her," he says, and then he runs.

Runs and runs. He runs past the shops. Runs across the parking lot of DJ's Liquors. Runs across the painted turtle and the circle racetrack. Across the railroad tracks. He trips on a fallen branch. Picks it up. He carries it like a club and keeps running. He runs all the way to the dark and still park, where no one swings or slides because the whole world is watching the fireworks. The slide shimmers in the moonlight.

Tall Boy catches up to him, breathing hard.

"Cooper," Tall Boy says, chugging and panting, "they want to be left alone." He leans on the lid of a yellow metal garbage can to catch his breath. "Trust me. I feel left out too."

"But how can I know she is safe if I can't find her?"

"Safe?" Tall Boy says. "Oh, Cooper." Tall Boy says *Cooper* the way Caddie says *Cooper*—with all hope lost in the long "ooo."

Behind him, in the dark, comes a sound. A distant giggle. Caddie's laugh.

"See?" Tall Boy still gasps for air. "I told you."

"How can you be sure?"

Tall Boy drops to the ground. "Because."

Cooper drops his stick.

Fireworks ka-thunk and shoot through the air.

Another laugh. Then a loud, "C'mon."

"No," Caddie says. "Help me."

Help me. Help me. Help me. Cooper's whole body surges with worry.

"Did you hear that?" he says. "She's in danger. She's calling for help. We have to help her."

Tall Boy looks up at Cooper. His eyes are shiny. Like new quarters. He picks up the stick and runs toward the voices. Into the dark. Cooper runs behind Tall Boy. He runs until he sees The Grinner's silhouette. His white teeth glow like fangs in the moonlight.

"No way!" Caddie yells.

"Todd!" Tall Boy shouts. Then stops. He winds up, gathers his strength, and throws the stick. Like a dart, sharp and accurate, it hits The Grinner in the stomach. Knocks him to his knees.

Tall Boy is the hero. A knight in shining armor.

The Grinner moans. "Mike? That you? What gives?"

"It's time to go home."

"What's going on?" Caddie says from thin air.

Cooper turns and turns, searching for Caddie.

The Grinner stands. "You . . . ," he growls at

Tall Boy, but he doesn't finish his sentence. He jumps into the air and lands on Tall Boy. Takes him down. Tall Boy and The Grinner roll side to side like wrestling bears. Slaps and groans seem louder than the fireworks. A single punch. Tall Boy's fist to The Grinner's jaw. The Grinner coughs and spits.

Cooper wants to stomp. Wants to count. Wants to wash. But he must find Caddie.

The Grinner stops fighting. Stands like a question mark. Stands like Mr. Bell, crumpled and weak.

"What's with you lately?" The Grinner says.

"With *me?*" Tall Boy says. "What's with *you?*" He spits on the ground.

"Where's Caddie?" Cooper says. "Caddie!" he calls.

"Up here," Caddie says.

Cooper looks up. Caddie sits on a giant tree limb hanging over their heads. Her eyes blink in the darkness like stars. Her white dress puffs like a cloud. "I can't get down."

Fireworks ka-thunk, whistle, and rain in the sky. Pop and rain. Pop and rain. Crackle, ka-thunk, pop, and rain. Ka-thunk and spew.

The grand finale.

"C'mon, Todd. We better get back. My dad's probably looking for us," Tall Boy says.

"I'll get my own ride," The Grinner says. "From a friend." He limps into the woods like a wounded animal.

Tall Boy stands under the tree branch and looks up at Caddie. "I'll help you down," he says.

"I don't want your help," Caddie says. "I'll get down by myself."

"I thought you needed help," Tall Boy says.

"Not from you," Caddie says. "And I'll get my own ride too."

Tall Boy. He is different from The Grinner. "Mike is not the foe," Cooper says.

"So what," Caddie says. "What are you doing here anyway?"

"You were in danger. I came to your rescue." Cooper leans against the trunk of the big tree.

"I don't need to be rescued, Cooper. I just need to get down. And I'm not going to jump from way up here."

"I'll get Mom."

"No!"

Cooper scans the pitch-black park. Spots the garbage can. Points. "I'll get that old garbage can."

Now Mike is nowhere in sight. Cooper turns. Searches the darkness. Turns again. And there he is. At the edge of the park. Watching. Watching to make sure everything is okay. Mike watches him make sure the lid is on tight before Cooper pushes the garbage can to its side. Watches him roll it beneath the tree. Watches as he uses all his might to turn it right side up again.

Caddie reaches with her legs. Lands on the lid of the garbage can with a clunk. Cooper holds her hand. Helps her jump to the ground. "Your breath smells like Dad's," he tells her.

"Don't tell Mom," Caddie whispers. "Promise?"

Promise, promise, promise. "I promise," Cooper says. "But I don't think you should ever do that again."

Mike is still there. A shadow at the edge of the woods. Still watching. Then he turns and disappears across the train tracks.

Car engines start. Headlights come on. Cooper and Caddie walk along the edge of the parking lot. *Don't tell Mom. Don't tell Mom. Don't tell Mom.*

Caddie still holds Cooper's hand. Their mother leans against the van. Waiting.

"I'll ride home with you guys," Caddie says. She lets go of Cooper's hand.

"Sounds good," their mother says. "How was the dance?"

"Great," Cooper says.

"How would you know?" Caddie says.

Their mother laughs. "Caddie?"

"Great," Caddie says.

"You missed the grand finale, Cooper," his mother says. She hands Cooper the folded-up fishing blanket.

"No, I didn't," he says. He gets into the van and they ride home in the dark, watching far-off fireworks light up the sky above the tops of pointy black trees. Silently.

He writes in his lap, in the dark.

Taking risks and avoiding risks can be very confusing.
Sometimes they are the same.

In his room, Cooper picks up the small pale rock and hugs it to his chest. He is glad the big dark rock is at home. Alone. Glad The Father does not know about this night. He gives Amicus a food nugget. "Tonight I was almost as brave as you, little fella." And then he realizes That Boy wasn't there. That Boy didn't try to help him. He writes this in his notebook:

It is hard to know if you are doing the right thing.

Especially if you have to do it alone.

Cooper pictures the fireworks. The ka-thunk, whistle, and spew. He thinks of the grand finale. Thinks of Caddie's white eyes, like stars in the sky. The brightest novae. He crawls under the covers, safe in Grandpa's bed, and opens *Inferno*.

Where. Where. Where. We. We. We. Came. Came. Came . . . Where we came forth and once more saw the stars. The. The. The. End. End. End. The end. The end. The end.

Across the lake, icy rain sparkles in the sky.

Cooper has definitely seen the stars. And now he has finished his grandfather's good and famous book. He is done. He has read it all, every sentence, every paragraph, every page, three times three. But the world is still not safe. Caddie has had a close call.

Cooper flips the pages of *Inferno* back to the beginning.

And starts over.

FRIENDS

Caddie lies in the sun. Her body is shiny like the foil landing strip on Tezorene, the molten planet where there is no garbage. Everything can be pushed to its center, melted, and reused. All food is served piping hot. The magnificent structure includes a factory for spaceships made of shells and acorns.

Cooper sings the national anthem of this great orb and its kind Tezornaut people. "O Tezorene, where no one's mean . . ." He holds the red bucket at the shallow shore of the lake.

"Cooper," Caddie says.

He cringes at the first sound, the extra-hard C of his name. Caddie wants to tell him something. Something he knows will singe his feelings. But he doesn't turn around.

"I know there's no planet called Tezorene," he says. "I just made it up."

"I wasn't going to say that."

Cooper freezes. His heart beats hot. Hotter than the sun on Tezorene. He waits for Caddie to speak. But he doesn't want to know what he has done wrong. He is trying hard to be good. So hard his brain hurts with trying.

Cooper steps back from the shore. From a hilltop on Tezorene, he squints at a different galaxy. A sun pierces the ozone, burns through the atmosphere, and shines through the treetops to a beach. The otherworldly sun shines on a boy named Cooper who holds a red bucket full of water and shivers. The boy named Cooper is an alien being. No one understands the message he brings to helpless Earthlings.

"About the other night," Caddie says. "At the fireworks."

Cooper pours the bucket of water across the lands of Tezorene so his feet will not burn. The sand mounds slide low, like liquid lava, and melt into the earth. "Did I embarrass you one more time?"

Caddie laughs. "Yes, you did. But it's okay. This time, anyway. Todd's cute, but he's not my type."

"I tried to warn you, my lady," Cooper says.

"I guess. If you want to call it that. But, Cooper?"

The sand grows hotter beneath Cooper's feet. Tezorene is shifting on its axis. *Don't tell Mom. Don't tell Mom. Don't tell Mom.* "I didn't tell Mom," he says.

"That's good because that's what I'm trying to tell you. You need to mind your own business."

Cooper is braced for more. Braced for catastrophe. And shame. "What else?" his heart beats like the fireworks. *Ka-thunk. Ka-thunk. Ka-thunk.*

"Nothing," she says. "That's enough. For now."

Cooper's heart breathes. "Okay," he says. He hurries to the lapping shore for more water. "O, Tezorene, Tezorene . . ."

A black dot on the horizon grows out of the water like time-lapsed photography. Egg, larva, bug. Bigger, blacker, bobbing. Cooper sets down the bucket. Cups his hand to his brow. "What's that?"

Caddie sits up in the sun. Evens out her beach towel. Tugs at her bathing suit and looks across the lake, squinting. "Maybe it's the Loch Ness Monster."

Cooper thinks of The Grinner. Of the smashed castle. Of Amicus the Great. Of Caddie's white eyes in the dark. "It could be," he says when he returns to Tezorene with a bucket of water. "You said he lives on the lake."

First Caddie says, "What?" and then she says, "Cooper! How did you know Todd lives on the lake?" She lies back down with a big *harrumph*. "You *were* listening, weren't you? I knew it. See what I mean? You have to mind your own business. For a lot of reasons."

Cooper watches the growing bug cross the lake. Bigger and blacker. A boat maybe. Zooming toward them. Who is it? Who would be coming to their cabin? What would they want? He stomps his right foot one, two, three times. Stomps his left foot, one, two . . .

"Don't, Cooper. You've been doing so well."

"But I don't know who it is."

"That's because we don't know who anybody is up here. We might as well be the last people left on Earth." Caddie rolls to her back.

"What if we are?" Cooper says.

"Cooper!"

The black orb persists, bigger yet. A fancy fishing boat guided so carefully, so slowly, it barely leaves a wake. The boat hums smoothly, makes a beeline for the dock. A tall boy with dark hair mans the steering wheel, standing up. "I think it's the Earthling known as Mike," Cooper says.

Caddie pops back up. "Are you sure?"

Cooper bows toward his sister. "Do not worry, my lady. He is the safe one. And he travels alone."

"Cooper! What did I just say?"

"Ahoy!" Mike calls from the boat. The motor sputters. Shuts off in a cloud of exhaust. Mike leaps to the dock. Loops a rope around a stanchion like a pro. "Mind if I come ashore?"

"You already did," Cooper says.

"Cooper, shh!" Caddie says. She pulls a T-shirt on over her swimsuit.

"Hi," Mike says, stepping off the dock into the sand.

"Hi," Caddie says.

"Ahoy," Cooper says.

Mike carries something small in one hand, swings the other. "I brought you a present."

"A gentleman with a gift for a lady," Cooper says. He bows toward Mike. "I approve."

"Cooper," Caddie whispers, "I'm warning you."

A pink wave, like fresh sunburn, sears Mike's dotted cheeks. Stops at the black shadow beneath Mike's right eye. Mike has a black eye. A battle scar. "No, it's for you, Cooper. It's a book."

"For me?" Cooper stands taller.

Caddie strains to see the cover.

"I mean, you can read it too, Caddie, if you want." He holds out a curled paperback book. Its cover is torn. "Have you read it?"

"*The Adventures of Tom Sawyer*," Cooper says. He reaches for the book. "No, but I have heard it is a good and famous book. How did you know?"

"Know what?"

"I have been wanting to read another work of classic literature."

Mike's lips try to form words, but nothing comes out. He looks at Caddie and then at his feet. He puts his hands in his pockets. Kicks at an acorn in the sand. "It's my all-time favorite. I figured if we both like Dante, you'd like Mark Twain too."

"Mark Twain is his *nom de plume*," Cooper says. "His real name is Samuel Langhorne Clemens."

"I know," Mike says. He frowns before he smiles.

"We had to read it in school last year," Caddie says. "I don't know, Cooper. I think it might be too old for you."

"It is not a very big book," Cooper says.

"But it might have things you're not ready to understand."

"I can read anything you put in front of me."

"Reading and understanding aren't the same. Besides, times were different way back then, Coop. People treated people differently. Unfairly. And called them names."

Names, Cooper thinks. Like "That Boy" and "Weirdo." Times are the same now. He pulls his notebook from his pocket. Holds it against the book. Writes quickly.

> People are like bugs. They start out small, grow bigger, and fly away.
> They all look different until you look at them closely.
> And then you can see they are mostly the same.

Mike is quiet. He kicks at the sand. "But it's about friends too," he says. "Unlikely friends. And their adventures."

"I see that," Cooper says. "It says so on the cover."

"Next thing you know, you'll want to build a raft and sail away." Mike winks at him. Smiles. "That's what I always wanted to do when I was your age." Then Mike looks at Caddie. Caddie is picking at her flaking hot-pink nail polish. When she looks up, Mike looks away.

Cooper squeezes the book. Presses his toes into the sand. The last thing he will ever want to do is build a raft and sail away. He holds the book tight. Keeps it shut. He does not want to see the words. Does not want to read the words three times three in front of Mike.

Mike is waiting.

Caddie sighs, more bored than ever. "Say thank you, Cooper."

"Thank you, Cooper."

Mike laughs, but Caddie frowns. She does not like stupid jokes.

"Finish the book and I'll take you fishing. I know all the best spots." Mike turns to Caddie. "Maybe you'll come too."

Fishing? Not fishing. Never fishing. Ever. "Caddie doesn't like to fish," Cooper says.

"Cooper!"

Mike puts his hands on his hips. "You spend your summers on the lake and you don't like to fish?"

"She's a girl," Cooper says.

Mike laughs. A short burst of a laugh.

Caddie kicks sand at Cooper. Suddenly a sand-storm swirls over Tezorene. "Ow!" Caddie yells. She blinks and stands up. Presses her fingers to her eye.

"Don't rub it or you'll abrade the cornea!" Cooper shouts.

"Cooper!" Caddie blinks wildly, then closes her sore eye again. She wraps her towel around her hips, hurries across the hot sand.

"It's true! I read it in a book!" Cooper shouts up the hill. Caddie is silent except for small sticks snapping beneath her feet. "Ow," she says again.

Cooper turns his back to Mike. But just for a second.

It is hard to mind your own business if you think you can be of help to someone.

"I better get back to work," Mike says. He watches Caddie disappear over the top of the hill. Shrugs his shoulders. "I hope your eye's okay!" he shouts.

Caddie doesn't answer. Mike's face is splotchy red again. As red as a bloodshot eye.

"Maybe she got sand in her ears too," Cooper says.

Mike laughs again. Stops laughing. Pretends he didn't laugh at all. He picks up a small rock, throws it at the lake. The rock touches down one, two, three times. Cooper picks up a rock. He curves his arm like

Mike's, swings the rock at the lake. It climbs high and falls. Drops straight to the bottom of the lake.

"You gotta hold your arm straight," Mike says. "Throw the rock across the top of the lake. Skim it. Kind of like a jet ski."

Cooper has never ridden a jet ski. He picks up another rock. Holds his arm straight. When he throws this rock into the air, it plops like a dropped fish.

"It has to be a flat rock if you want it to skip," Mike says. "Look for a flat rock."

Cooper looks at the ground. He doesn't want to skip rocks anymore. He can't make a rock skim the lake like a jet ski and he doesn't want to practice in front of Mike. "Where do you work?" he asks.

"My dad's bait shop on North Bay. By all the other shops. Where else?"

Where else? Where else? Where else? Cooper would like to ask Mike more important questions, but he doesn't know what to say. He doesn't know how to talk to Mike. He thinks of the Tezornauts on Tezorene. Knows he is an alien being. Knows he would need an interpreter to communicate on their planet.

"See ya 'round," Mike says.

"Okay," Cooper says.

Mike walks down the dock to the boat. Yanks the rope from the stanchion.

"Hey, Mike!" Cooper yells. "Thanks for the book."

"Sure, Cooper." The motor starts quietly, with one smooth pull. Mike waves and turns the boat seaward.

"Hey, Mike!" Cooper yells one more time. "See ya 'round."

Mike waves again, without looking. A ripple follows the stern, and Mike gets smaller and smaller until Mike and the ripple disappear and all that is left of Mike is *The Adventures of Tom Sawyer* in Cooper's sweaty hands.

Cooper carries the book into the cabin. Into the kitchen, where he hears noises. Caddie holds her head under the pump, blinking and blinking and blinking. Water spills across her cheek, splashes on the counter. Splatters Cooper. "I think he likes you," Cooper says.

"I think he likes *you*," Caddie says.

"Me?"

Cooper hopes Mike does like him. Hopes that this is the most believable thing Caddie has ever said in her whole life.

Cooper fans the pages of his new good and famous book. He thinks of Mike's red cheeks. And his black eye. He remembers the big stick, and Mike's fight with The Grinner. And today, Mike's shrugged shoulders. And sand in Caddie's ears. Cooper and Mike have a private joke between them.

Sometimes you make friends when you least expect them.

By accident. Like getting sand in your eye.

Cooper isn't sure about reading *The Adventures of Tom Sawyer*. He wishes the new good and famous book were a guidebook to how friends work.

TRICHOPTERA

Caddie hops out of the van as soon as they pull up in front of the grocery store. "You're coming with me, Cooper," his mother says.

But Cooper doesn't want to go grocery shopping. He doesn't want to see the rows of milk and grapefruit today. He doesn't feel up to the spices and soups that might be out of order. It's too much work. His mother moves so quickly, it's hard to keep up. And if he can't keep up, something terrible might happen. "I don't want to go with you," he says.

"Don't think you're coming with me," Caddie calls over her shoulder as she crosses the street.

His mother sighs. "What do you want to do, Cooper?"

Cooper looks at the sign boards up and down the street—the candy shop, the souvenir shop,

"Moccasins Sold Here," Ron's Bait Shop. Ron. Mike. Cooper feels a small smile appear on his face. All by itself. He pulls his notebook from his pocket.

Smiles are like dandelions growing between two rocks.
They cannot be stopped.

"There." Cooper points at the sign, Ron's Bait Shop. "I'm going there." He looks left, looks right, looks left again. He lets the red van pass before he crosses the street.

A tiny bell tinkles overhead when he opens the door to Ron's Bait Shop. The store is a library of messy things. The shelves are tall, busy, and green. Cooper closes his eyes. The air smells like a storm. He has been here before. With his grandfather. He remembers the clock on the wall with leaping fish for hands. *Tick. Tick. Tick.*

"Hey! How's it going? How do you like *Tom Sawyer?*"

Cooper opens his eyes. "I reckon I do," he says. "Done started last night."

"Should I call you Tom from now on?"

Cooper shakes his head.

Mike smiles. "How far are you?"

The words and the lines and the pages appear like a memory of a dream. *I, I, I. Reckon, reckon, reckon. There, there, there. I reckon there ain't one boy in a thousand, maybe two thousand that can do it the way it's got to be done. Aunt Polly, Aunt Polly, Aunt Polly.* "Not very far," Cooper says.

Mike sits on a tall stool at the counter. His hands are busy. *Busy, busy, busy.* Cooper moves closer. "What are you doing?"

"Tying flies."

Cooper knows of this craft. He has seen the instructions in a book. Mike is making fake bugs called trichoptera. Sticky bugs with wings like tissue paper that sputter across still water like tiny raindrops. Grandpa's book on fishing in Colorado says fish like to eat them. "You have an infestation," Cooper says, pointing at the pile of finished bugs on the counter. "Of caddis flies."

"You know your bugs," Mike says. He wraps a hook with wire, then with delicate thread. He twists and ties and clips, like a robot. Dabs one end with clear fingernail polish.

"Caddie has some of that," Cooper says.

Mike's eyes blink fast and blink again before he

smiles. "How's her eye?" he asks. He puts another bug in the pile.

"I believe she has made a full recovery," Cooper says.

"Can you say hi to her for me?"

"I reckon I can," Cooper says.

A bell tinkles every time the door opens, and Mike glances up. Says hi. Every time. Then he wraps, ties, plucks another bit of hair and fur, wraps some more and ties. Clips. Pulls another length of thread. Wraps and ties.

"I thought fly fishing was a sport of the mountain streams," Cooper says.

"Mountain streams and Minnesota quarries. They stock 'em with trout."

"You mean it's pretend?"

Mike whispers, "Don't tell anyone. It'll just be our little secret."

"Really?"

Mike's busy fingers stop. "Oh, no," he says. "They know. I mean, I was just kidding about the secret." Cooper looks away. He does not see the point in pretend fishing.

A motor hums and water gurgles. It sounds like a radio left on in a different room. Cooper tracks it down. The hum comes from a black box next to a big claw-foot tub in the corner. The black box is a pump that circulates water around and around in the tub. Cooper peers into the water. Into the churning water where the minnows swim in circles. Plastic buckets full of black dirt hang from the rolled edge of the tub on twisted black coat hangers. Cooper wants to turn off the motor. Stop the whir. Set the minnows free.

Suddenly, That Boy is standing next to him. Cooper hasn't seen him in hours and hours and hours. He thought he left him behind at the cabin. He touches the twisted wire. Cooper does not want to count the hangers. But That Boy needs to count them. One, two, three . . .

The bell tinkles.

Cooper is saved. He puts his hand in his pocket.

"Hi, Mike," a voice says. The customer is an old man. Like his grandpa. But not as old as Mr. Bell. His bulky vest has a hundred pockets, and Cooper thinks of all the things he could carry in those pockets: his rocks, magnifying glass, maybe even Amicus. Pencils. His notebook. And books. A vest just like it hangs high in the window.

It doesn't really have a hundred pockets, but a

vest with a hundred pockets is a happy thought. And Cooper needs a happy thought. Right now.

"Hey, Jack. How's it going? Any big ones yet?" Mike asks.

"Nope. But I'm not giving up."

Jack shops the row of fishing rods. Lifts one and bounces the rod. Spins the reel. Puts it back in the rack where it belongs. "Thought I'd try some soft-hackle caddis this time."

"Got 'em right here. Can't tie 'em fast enough." Mike nods at the growing pile of caddis flies on the counter.

"And some night crawlers," Jack says. "For my grandson."

The bell tinkles again. "You got fishing licenses?" the big man in the orange cap asks.

"Sure do," Mike says. "Hey, Cooper, can you help me while I write this up?"

Cooper stands over the pool of minnows, watching. Watching the minnows swim their circles. He feels the rhythm. Up, down, and back. Knows the repetition. Senses their fear. One minnow drifts low in the tub. Rolls with the fake tide. That minnow is dead. Like his grandfather. Nothing you can do about it now.

"Cooper? Can you get Jack here some night crawlers?"

"Sure," Cooper says, but he doesn't know why he says sure. He doesn't know how to get night crawlers in Ron's Bait Shop. He imagines himself in the dark earth beneath the cabin where the water drains from the pump at the kitchen sink. He is the night crawler. Crawling. Hurrying. Curling into a ball.

Afraid.

That Boy won't leave. And he won't leave Cooper alone. He counts the minnows, but they swim so fast he can't keep up. One, two, three . . . Upstream, downstream. He loses track. Starts over. One, two, three . . .

"Cooper?" Mike stands next to him. Whispers, "The night crawlers are in the buckets." Mike sinks his hand into the plastic bucket. Pulls out mud that squirms and seethes. "See?" He reaches for a small cardboard box. Counts out twelve giant worms that duck from the light and wrap around his fingers. The worms are holding on for dear life. He pushes them off, closes the lid.

Cooper wants to wash. Wants to count. *Please*, he whispers to That Boy. *Not in front of Mike.* He remembers what Caddie said. *Be polite.* Remembers how badly he needs a friend. Cooper shakes his head. "No, thank you, Mike. I prefer the fake flies." He stands by the counter. Picks up a fire-red fly from a different pile. Rolls it back and forth with his fingertip.

"Where's your dad today?" Jack says.

Mike rings up Jack's soft-hackle caddis flies and night crawlers. "Over at DJ's. They had another break-in."

"Have you guys been hit this summer?" Jack asks.

Mike shakes his head. Counts out change from Jack's twenty-dollar bill. "Not yet."

"Must be a bigger market for beer than there is for worms," Jack says and laughs at his own joke. "I hope I don't have to come back for any more woolly buggers." Jack laughs again. Jack is happy. The bell tinkles. Jack is gone. *Gone fishin'.* Cooper laughs in his mind at his stupid joke. A Tom Sawyer joke. But only for a second. He cannot forget what he is doing.

Watching. Waiting. Ready.

Always.

Mike's hands are busy again. *Busy, busy, busy.* Cooper is drawn to the fake lures like a hungry fish. "Maybe I could do that," Cooper says. He picks up a hook and a piece of wire and wraps the wire around the hook in concentric circles. Methodically. Tediously. Wonderfully. The rows are as even as the spindle of wire on Grandpa's workbench.

He pulls brown thread. Ties and wraps. Ties and clips. He reaches for a bit of fur. Mike nods. Cooper concentrates. Feels his tongue pointed against his upper lip. Just like Mike's, his hands are busy. *Busy, busy, busy.*

But his mind is not busy. His mind feels loose and free. And That Boy has nothing to do. That Boy is bored. Cooper imagines his heavy brain turned to liquid. Draining out through his opened mouth— That Boy sliding out with all the muck. Leaving room for ideas. Ideas as soft as the clouds. He imagines himself floating across the sky.

The caddis fly is perfect.

"Wow!" Mike says.

"I'm a fast learner."

"Maybe, but you better pick up some speed if you want to make any money at it."

"Money?" Cooper says. "You mean, like a job?"

"Yeah, like a job. I'll pay you to tie flies. Maybe you can buy something you've always wanted."

Cooper knows what he would like to buy. But he has not always wanted it. He has never wanted it until this moment. He points up high at the window—at the giant vest that does not really have a hundred pockets. "I will want to buy that."

"And then I'll take you fishing," Mike says.

No. Not fishing. Never fishing. Ever.

Cooper picks up another piece of wire.

Busy, busy, busy.

Free, free, free.

SADNESS

Cooper sits on the sofa in the golden cabin light, tying caddis flies. He dabs nail polish on the seventy-seventh fly and sets it on a cookie tray to dry.

"Dad called," his mother says as she walks from the kitchen to the dining room. "He plans to be here this weekend." She goes back and forth, from the kitchen to the dining room, carrying knick-knacks and the toaster and the pitcher and the dead ivy from the grandfather's funeral and all the things that get dusty and leave rings on the kitchen counter, and sets them on the dining room table. One by one. She empties drawers, sorts junk. She is giving the kitchen a good Irish scrub, just like her grandmother used to say.

"Do you think he'll really come this time?" Caddie asks.

The question scares Cooper. He waits, afraid of the answer. He thinks of the big rock at home alone on his desk and wonders if the rocks in his room, here, up north at the cabin, miss that big rock. He is certain the big rock likes being alone.

"I think so," their mother says. "His biggest project of the year is finally behind him."

"I'll bet you fifty dollars he can't make it," Caddie says.

Cooper watches his mother's face for a smile. "We'll see," she says. No smile.

Cooper picks up a piece of wire. The last piece. He needs more supplies. He wraps, ties, and clips and puts the last caddis fly on the cookie tray. When they are dry, he will put them in the box for Mike. He opens *The Adventures of Tom Sawyer.* Reads. Reads and listens to Caddie and his mother.

Scissors clink. Caddie sighs. She measures, cuts, and peels shelf paper to line the drawers. "Have I been grounded or something?"

"No, I just need the help," Cooper hears his mother say.

"Why can't Cooper help?" Caddie says. "He's good at this sort of thing."

Cooper knows the answer. Knows his mother

will not let him help because he will measure the drawers perfectly—the way they should be measured. She doesn't like perfect things. Perfect things take too much time. And because she knows Cooper might put the junk in his room for safekeeping. Cooper thinks about Mr. Bell's garage. He thinks about Mr. Bell and the ice cream. He thinks about Jack's big vest and how he would never need drawers with one hundred pockets.

Cooper reads about a graveyard. About warts. He has been so busy tying flies he has missed this good and famous book full of adventures. Except for the part about the dead cat. Dead. Kaput. Nothing you can do about it. Tom Sawyer makes friends with Huckleberry Finn. Huckleberry Finn sounds like another fake fly to tie.

A drawer slams shut in the kitchen. "Now can I go?" Caddie pleads. Pleads a dying wish. No, not dying. Cooper wants to unthink that word, *dying*. He must read. Read to expunge that thought. Read to save Caddie from the flames. He should not have been tying flies. He should have been reading. Reading three times three to protect his mother and Caddie and Amicus and the world.

Caddie moans so loudly a loon calls to her from

the lake. Cooper puts his finger on the word *Finn*.
Listens to the lonely loon. Listens to the clinks in the
kitchen. He is glad to know Caddie is alive and well.
Finn. Finn. Finn.

A drawer slams shut. "There. Done. That's the
last one," Caddie says.

"Help me put everything back and then you're
free," his mother says.

From the corner of his eye, Cooper watches
Caddie in the dining room. When she picks up the
dead ivy, her movements jerk and stall. Cooper turns
his head. Watches as Caddie moves and thinks in
stop motion. Like a pixilated movie. Her eyes blink.
Her fingers touch the green tape. Cooper knows he
cannot stop what she is thinking. Cannot stop what
will happen next.

His stomach is in free fall.

Spilling through the stratosphere.

Caddie holds the fishing boat with the dead ivy
in front of her curious eyes. She squints. Shakes
her head with disbelief. "Mom," she says, poking a
purple fingernail at the little green stem. Her small
laugh puffs the air. "This plant is dead." She tugs at
the stem. Unwinds a piece of green tape.

The dead plant grows.

Cooper watches as his mother reaches for the pot. "No, it's not. See? It's still green. It'll come back."

"Mom, look. It's just green wire wrapped with florist tape."

His mother looks again. She cannot believe her eyes. Or her ears. But Cooper knows she realizes everything Caddie says is getting more and more believable every day. She takes the pot in one hand, touches her lips with the other. She stands as still and lifeless as the green wire.

Cooper pictures his grandfather under water. Sees himself dive to the bottom of the lake to save him. He wants to catch the ivy in a freefall. Wants to pick up his mother and carry her to Tezorene, where everyone lives full to the brim with happiness. Where sadness is not allowed.

"It's my fault," Cooper says. "I forgot to water it." He runs to the kitchen. Gets the antique pitcher, pumps the water, fills it to the brim. He hurries to his mother's side. "It's all my fault," he says again.

"No, it isn't," Caddie says. "It's looked like that for months."

"It has?" their mother says. She sits down. The fishing boat shakes in her hand.

Cooper can see his mother filling with holes. She is emptying out. Caving in. He must hurry to refill her.

He tilts the pitcher and the little fishing boat fills with water, overflows into his mother's lap. She shivers. And laughs. But Cooper knows she is not cold and her laugh is not happy. She sets the plant on the dining room table. Wipes the droplets, like tears, with her hand. "It's just a plant," she says and laughs again. "What was I thinking?"

Hope, hope, hope. Cooper knows she was thinking about hope. And it's all his fault her hope is gone. He has let her down. Cooper watches his mother closely for small cracks and signs of fire. For embers in her heart.

His mother laughs tiny little disappearing laughs until she no longer makes a peep of sound. She puts the ivy back on the windowsill in the kitchen and presses a towel against her wet jeans. "I've been thinking about planting a vegetable garden," she says. Her voice buckles beneath the weight of her heavy heart.

"That sounds great, Mom," Caddie says.

"Just some tomatoes and green beans," his mother says. "What do you think, Cooper?"

Cooper pictures his calendar. Calculates the time. "We have thirty-two days left at the cabin. I believe—"

"Cooper," Caddie says, frowning.

Cooper listens carefully to the hard C of his name. Caddie is warning him. He picks up his book and goes to his room. Flips his notebook to a clean page and writes.

Sometimes it is hard to say the right words.
To keep track of thoughts and facts and truth.
And hope.

Before he closes his notebook, he writes this down too:

Sometimes your brain plays tricks on your eyes, making you believe in impossible things.

And one more thing:

Some people think sadness is the opposite of happiness, but that is not true.
Sadness is the opposite of hope.

And this:

Sadness is a bully. It steals your happiness away when you aren't looking.
Sadness butts in line and makes hope go last.
If hope ever gets a chance at all.

Cooper lays out his rocks on his bed, touches them one by one. He thinks about Mr. Bell all alone in the hospital. He will make him ice cream when he comes home. He gives Amicus an extra food nugget because the frog has so little to look forward to.

And then he reads. He reads to Caddie's mean frown. To his mother's glistening eyes. To The Father's phone calls. To Amicus the Great's solitary existence. (Maybe someday Cooper will find another tadpole, like Amicus, and Amicus will have a friend too.) He reads to the truth of the dead ivy. Reads to rid everyone of their sadness. To the secrets he must keep. To the loss of hope.

He reads every word three times, every line three times, and every page three times because today disaster came so close. So very close. As close as a last breath. He reads *The Adventures of Tom Sawyer* until he bumps into a mean word. Caddie is right. He does not understand. And he is worried about his species.

Being a human being can be very confusing.

Now Cooper needs to read to rid the world of all its meannesses and its sadnesses. But he cannot read the mean words three times three. Cannot read those words at all.

He closes his eyes and glides his finger on the page. He pictures himself as a period at the end of a sentence. A tiny dot in the universe. He can see as plain as day that Cooper Cameron is a minuscule problem in a very, very big world.

HOPE

Cooper's eyes are still closed when Caddie knocks on his door.

"Put your bathing suit on, Cooper. It's summer. We're going down to the beach. Mom says."

Cooper puts on his bathing suit. Tucks his secret notebook into the secret pocket of his bathing suit. Says goodbye to Amicus.

Caddie smears sunblock on him like soap, head to toe. The coconut oil she spreads on her arms and legs makes her glimmer like a wet seashell.

"It's so hot out," she says, tiptoeing across the mossy yard, side-stepping sticks and acorns.

Cooper follows, scanning the path for toads and beetles and other creatures he can rescue from the mean and scary world. Creatures that might like to inhabit Tezorene.

"Ow, ow, ow," Caddie says, hurrying across the hot sand to stand in the dark circle of shade beneath the birch tree.

"I wish we had something to float on," she says. "Even blow-up rafts. That would be kind of fun, wouldn't it?"

When Cooper shakes his head, he feels Caddie's eyes follow his head as it turns from one side to the other and back again.

Caddie lays her beach towel out on the sand. "You're scared of the water, aren't you, Coop?"

Caddie is right. She is always right. But she doesn't need to know this truth. He shakes his head again. Faster now, harder, so she won't misunderstand.

Caddie lies down on her stomach. Her hands under her chin. "Yes, you are. But I don't get it."

"A person can drown in less than one inch of water," he says. "I read it in a book on water safety."

"But you used to go swimming all the time, remember? Remember how Grandpa used to play Marco Polo with us? And tag? And then he'd have to drag you out of the water when it was time for bed. You'd get so cold your whole body was blue and shaking."

Yes, he remembers. Of course, he remembers. He can picture Grandpa in his baggy swimming trunks. Tying the strings across his big belly. Like yesterday, he can see Grandpa carrying his fishing gear to the boat. Dragging the old wooden fishing boat out of the boathouse. His prized possession. In Cooper's mind, the rusty wheels of the boat trailer screech like a flock of frantic pigeons.

"I am wiser now," Cooper says. His eyes shift from the boathouse to the stretch of blue in front of him. He stares, watching every molecule of water glint in the sun.

"Maybe you read too much."

What Caddie says is not a joke, but it is funny. Still, he cannot laugh.

"Would you do it for me?" Caddie asks.

"What?"

"Go swimming."

As if he is already under water, Cooper gasps for air. He is working hard to not embarrass Caddie one more time. He wants to make her happy. Protect her at all costs. But he cannot go swimming. Ever. "If you were drowning, I would save you."

Cooper slips his notebook from his secret pocket.

Sometimes you must do what scares you to help someone you love.

"Oh, Cooper." Caddie mounds sand under one end of her beach towel like a pillow. Lies down on her back. Closes her eyes. "I miss him too, you know."

"Dad?"

"Sure," she says. "But I meant Grandpa."

Cooper doesn't want to talk about Grandpa. He is dead. And there is nothing you can do about it now.

Except be sad.

And protect his mother.

And Caddie.

And Amicus.

And everything else that matters.

Because everything matters.

All the time.

Cooper crawls across the sand. Gathers acorns. He builds a parapet on a turret of Tezorene. Strengthens the fortification to protect the Tezornauts.

"Oh, my God," Caddie says. She sits up. "What's the date today?"

Cooper thinks. Pictures his calendar again. "It is July 25th."

"You know what that means?" Her voice worries Cooper. He watches her closely. "Today is the anniversary of Grandpa's death. No wonder Mom is so sad."

Cooper can't believe he didn't know. Can't believe he wasn't counting the days.

"Whatever you do, don't say anything to Mom," Caddie says.

Don't say anything to Mom. Don't say anything to Mom. Don't say anything to Mom.

Caddie lies back down on her sand pillow. "Remember when he'd tell us stories about helping his dad on the farm? Remember how the cow stepped on his foot? And how he put ice in a bucket and wore it to school like a shoe? He told that same story over and over again. I thought I was going to lose my mind."

Cooper crouches on the grounds of Tezorene, acorns in his hands.

Of course he remembers. All of it. Grandpa did everything the same over and over again. Covered his fried eggs with ketchup. Lit his pipe with a single puff. Shaved without a mirror, his chin pointed into the air. Roasted the marshmallows until they caught on fire. Told the same stories. Over and over again. The same way. Until they bored Caddie silly.

See ya later, alligator, Grandpa said.

In a while, crocodile, Cooper hollered back.

Every time. Every time they pulled out of the driveway and headed home.

Cooper sits. Thinks. Writes. Makes the letters as perfect as possible.

Sometimes the things that bore you silly are the same things that make you feel safe.

"It's not the same up here anymore. He always made everything better," Caddie says. "Especially . . ." Caddie stops talking.

A horse fly lands on Cooper's kneecap. He blows it into the air. "Especially what?" he says.

Caddie doesn't answer. Her face is scrunched, her lips and eyelids pressed together so hard their tiny muscles are shaking. A wet stripe runs from her eye. Tears collect in her ear.

Caddie is sad. As sad as his mother. Cooper's breaths go deeper and deeper and deeper, making room for more sadness. Caddie's and his mother's. Filling himself with their sadnesses is the only way he can help. He does not know how to make everything better the way Grandpa did. He wants to tell

Caddie to think happy thoughts, but he knows happy thoughts don't work. If Grandpa were here, he'd say, "There, there, Caddie-girl." He'd wrap his big arms around her and say the same thing over and over again. *It'll be okay. It'll be okay. It'll be okay.*

But Cooper isn't sure it will. And he cannot tell Caddie a lie.

So he doesn't say anything at all.

Caddie reaches for her T-shirt. Dabs at her face with its sleeve.

The sun is hot. Tezorene has melted. It must be rebuilt if the Tezornauts are to survive. They will need a new shelter where no one is allowed to be mean. Or sad. Cooper fills the red bucket with lake water at the shore. Pours the water on the ancient ruins of Tezorene.

"Do I make you sad too?" he asks. The words are hard to say. They catch in his throat like a horsefly in a spider web, but he knows the backs of his flailing words do not glisten in the sunlight.

Caddie sits up and tries to smile. "No, Coop. You just drive me crazy." She pulls her T-shirt over her head. "Not always. Just sometimes."

"What about Mom?"

Caddie shifts to her stomach, leans on her elbows.

Stares Cooper in the eyes. "I think it's more complicated than that," she says.

"Do you think he will ever come back?"

"Who?"

"Dad. I believe I scared him away."

"Just say *think*, Cooper. You *think* things happen. No one says, 'I believe.'" She sits up on her towel. Pounds her fake pillow. Sand sticks to her shiny legs. Her face is red, but not from the sun. "Besides, it's not your fault."

This time Cooper cannot believe her words. They can't be true. Perhaps Caddie has run out of all the things she knows to be true. Cooper knows he is at fault. Everything is his fault. "Why do you say that?"

"Because . . ." Caddie kneels next to Tezorene and grabs the red bucket. Fills it with wet sand. Packs it down with all her might. "Because sometimes things just happen. And because that stupid little plant isn't your fault either."

"But I was supposed to water it."

"Cooper, see? This is what I mean." Caddie holds her hands out like a preacher reaching for the congregation. Reaching for the believers.

Cooper is not a believer.

That Boy is not a believer either.

"Think of all the dead plants in the world. Were you supposed to water those? Think of hurricanes and floods. Are they your fault? Think of wars and cemeteries."

Cooper closes his eyes. "I do."

Caddie screams. Not a real scream. A fake scream.

He must write this down:

Sometimes fake things are worse than the real things they copy.

"I'm sorry," he says.

"But that's the whole problem, Cooper. You don't have to be sorry for everything. Especially for things you didn't do. It's not your fault." Caddie's voice quivers. He can't tell if she is mad. Or sad again. Or both.

"You have nothing to do with things that can't be helped. Or things that happened a hundred years ago. Or things that happen on the other side of the world."

"What about this side of the world?" he says.

When Caddie shakes her head, Cooper trembles with worry. Caddie doesn't understand. There is so much to think about. So much to worry about.

His mother and The Father. And mean words. And Caddie. And lost turtles. And lonely people. And endangered species. Missing children. And poor Mr. Bell. There is too much to worry about. And That Boy is thinking the same thing. His work is overwhelming. Grandpa died and it was all his fault. He can't let it happen again.

Cooper feels his hands reaching. Reaching into the air. Reaching for the water. The everlasting water . . .

"Cooper, don't do this."

But Cooper isn't listening. He scrubs his hands. Rubs them and turns them and turns them and rubs them.

"Cooper, I mean it."

His hands tumble over each other in the air. Sand scrapes between his fingers like crystalized soap.

"Please, Cooper."

But That Boy has taken over. Cooper cannot stop washing his hands in the air.

"Now you're driving me crazy, Cooper." Caddie grabs at his hands. Misses. Grabs again. She wraps Cooper's arms around the bucket. Squeezes her hands against his. Dumps the bucket full of sand upside down. She throws the bucket at the hill. Pats with Cooper's hands in hers. Makes him pat the mound of sand.

And then something changes inside her. He can feel it. She ignites like wildfire. She pats and pats with his hands. Slaps them harder and harder until the sand scrapes like razors against his skin. Scraping and scraping and scraping. She slaps the sand with his hands until his skin burns like fire.

But he does not make her stop. Does not say, "You're hurting me." He does not say anything. He knows she is trying to help him. And he needs all the help in the world. No, he cannot take all the help in the world. It isn't fair.

His eyes burn. He looks down so Caddie can't see his face. He knows she feels him shudder.

Caddie stops patting the sand with Cooper's hands. Stops in mid-air. "Oh, Cooper," she says. She puts her arms around him. "Cooper." She squeezes him until he cannot breathe. He does not cry out. He wants her to know he would die for her.

"I'm sorry," she says. "I'm so sorry."

He coughs. Gagged by boiling hot tears. "You didn't mean it."

"I don't know what I mean," she says.

Caddie lets go all at once. "Let me—" She sniffs

against the back of her hand. "Let me help you, Coop." Her voice wobbles. "Please let me help you. Get another bucket of water."

Cooper gets another bucket of water. And another. And another.

Caddie molds the wet sand like an artist. She helps him build towers and walls and bridges on Tezorene. They build and build and build.

Side by side, they build Tezorene bigger and better and taller than ever. Until it sparkles in the sun. Caddie has an idea. She makes Cooper sit still with his eyes shut. He can hear her run to the cabin. Hear the screen door squeak open and snap shut. Two times. Hear her run back down the hill.

"Keep 'em shut, Cooper."

He does. And he hears her dig and rip and slap. Over and over again. When he opens his eyes, Caddie is pouring water into a deep moat lined with plastic wrap.

"There is no water on Tezorene," he says.

"We'll call it lava," Caddie says. "Trust me. It will be okay."

He believes her.

He believes her.

He believes her.

Lava. Burning a thousand degrees hotter than his tears. When it cools, it will be as hard as a rock. A rock wall around Tezorene is a good idea. The Tezornauts will be safe. He will not have to worry about them.

Sometimes bad things can turn into good things.

REASONS

Cars, cars, cars. People, people, people. The parking lot at Ron's Bait Shop is busy on this Sunday morning. A yellow banner rippling across the big window reads:

FISHING CONTEST

A big scale and long tables stand by the door. Men in fishing vests, like Jack's, weigh their catch to see if they have won first prize. A fancy rod and reel hang from the awning on fishing line.

WIN THIS CUSTOM ROD AND REEL

Cooper squeezes through the gaps in the crowd outside, between the laughs and the "How've you been?"s and the smells of sweat and coffee and lake reeds, with a box of caddis flies in his arms like a secret treasure.

The little bell tinkles over his head. Inside, Cooper bumps into a line of customers leading from the door to the counter. The till chirps and slams. Chirps and slams. Cooper waits, squished against fishing rods. Mike waves him forward, opens the till, and gives him a twenty-dollar bill. Mike doesn't ask about Tom Sawyer. Does not look in the cardboard box and say the flies are beautiful. Does not say thank you.

Something is wrong with Mike. Mike is not Mike. Mike appears to be an alien being.

Mike hands Cooper a bag of supplies for at least a million more flies. No, not a million. That is an exaggeration. Chirp and slam. Mike rings up another customer. As soon as Cooper finishes this bag of supplies, he will have saved up enough money to buy a vest like Jack's.

Cooper opens the door to leave, glances back at the counter. Mike looks up. But he doesn't smile. Does not say goodbye. Cooper points at the vest in the window. Gives Mike a big thumbs-up. Mike nods and looks away. Cooper wishes there were a book called *Mike* because he is certain there is something he needs to know. The bell tinkles over his head as he leaves.

Outside, Mike's dad, Ron, wears big black sunglasses. He resembles a larval fly. "Wouldja look at this one?" Ron shouts. Cooper looks. Sees Jack in his vest, holding a big fish up in the air, way over his head. Its silvery tail twitches. Brushes Jack's shoulder. "Whadja use there, Jack?"

"Soft-hackle caddis," Jack says. "Bought 'em right here."

"Looks like you're the lucky man today," Ron says.

Cooper feels taller. Stands tall. Stands strong. Feels his cells dividing, making muscle and marrow. His mother is right. He is growing like a weed. Maybe one of his beautiful flies made Jack a lucky man. Cooper squeezes through the smelly crowd to the table to see Jack's luck up close.

Ron slaps the fish on the table. Water hits Cooper in the face. He blinks the splash away, sees the fish more clearly. Ron nods—a big, happy nod—the measuring tape pulled taut in his fingertips. "No question. Biggest one yet," Ron says.

Jack smiles. Takes off his fishing cap and scratches his gray head. "I'd say it's about time."

The big fish does not smile. It thwaps its tail. Bounces. Lands near the edge of the table. "Whoa!" Ron says. Both men hold it down. Like the fish is a bad guy on TV. Like he's a crazy person. Then the fish lies still. Afraid to move. It opens its mouth like a baby bird's.

Shuts. Opens. Shuts. Opens. The fish is trying to blow bubbles. But it cannot blow bubbles in the air. The fish stares into Cooper's eyes. Pleads. No, the fish is not trying to blow a bubble. It is trying to speak. Speak to Cooper. Cooper holds still. Listens. He can't hear the fish, but he knows what it is saying. *I am dying. Can you help me?* The tiny black eye glistens. Like his mother's eyes when she is sad or desperate. Like the grandfather's when he was dying.

Jack is lucky.

The fish is not.

The fish is dying and there is nothing you can do about it.

Cooper's breath quivers.

That Boy leans over Cooper's shoulder for a better look.

He wants to stomp.

Wants to run.

That Boy pushes Cooper through the crowd. Chases him across the parking lot, all the way to the grocery store, running as fast as he can to keep up. Cooper's mother is not in Aisle A. And she is not in Aisle B, where the soups are. Where the red and white cans stand in rows like multiplication tables. Like books on bookshelves. Like soldiers. Like military graves.

Nothing you can do. Nothing you can do. Nothing you can do.

That Boy yanks the bag of caddis fly supplies from Cooper's arms. Drops it to the floor. That Boy turns the soup labels to read their names. Faces them to the front. Moves the can of vegetable soup from the C's, from the very wrong place next to cream of celery to its perfect place at the end.

"Cooper!"

Cooper ignores his name because he cannot stop. That Boy won't let him stop. And he mustn't stop. Too many lives are at risk. Too many fish. Too many species. The world is not safe.

"Cooper!" His mother's voice. Again. And then his mother's hand tightens on his shoulder. Strong, like a wood clamp. "Cooper, stop it!" But he's almost done. The T's line up perfectly on the cans of tomato soup. "Cooper—" She stops before she says the next word. She cannot speak. Her wordless breath puffs against his neck.

Cooper doesn't have to turn around to see his mother's glistening eyes. The fish is dying and there is nothing he can do about it. Just like the fish, every living thing will die and there is nothing he can do about it. No matter how hard he works, he can't stop it. *No, no, no.* And he can't stop what he needs to do. That Boy won't give up. That Boy will never give up trying. He rubs his hands together. Scrubs his face. Reaches in the air to feel the water. Reaches high overhead.

Reaches and reaches.

Reaches for the everlasting clean water.

Until his mother grabs his right hand and squeezes it warm and tight. He feels her arms clench around him. As strong as Grandpa's. Hears her whisper into his hair, "It's okay, Cooper. It's okay." He feels his new, strong, growing muscles give up in her grasp. In her hug. In a big bear hug just like Grandpa's.

Cooper hears the silence in the store. The silence of people watching. The wonderful silence of his mother holding him. Tight, warm, safe. Without a care in the world. Except for him. That Boy. That

Boy is at the root of everything. Cooper looks down. Ashamed. Embarrassed. Tired. He does not want to be his mother's only care in the world. It is not fair.

"How about we go get some pepperoni pizza. And some ice cream," she whispers.

Ice cream. His legs shake. The ground shifts and sways. But he can walk. He feels a strength in his legs he does not remember. He picks up his bag of caddis fly supplies. He has the strength to stand in the check-out lane. The strength to carry one bag of groceries to the van. He can make it across the street. He can wave at Caddie's reflection in the store window, beneath the sign "Moccasins Sold Here." He can use his last bit of strength to call to her, "Guess what? We're getting ice cream." He can do all this to make his mother happy.

"Pizza for dinner first, Cooper."

Caddie looks at their mother. At Cooper. "Now?" Her face wrinkles with confusion. "Mom. It's, like, afternoon."

Their mother nods. A desperate nod. A code in their secret language.

"I guess. If you say so," Caddie says.

They sit outside in the sunshine at the Pizza Pie and I shop. Caddie puts her bag in the empty chair.

Sits down first at the round green table with a million diamond-shaped holes in its top. It tilts every time Caddie leans on her elbows. Cooper doesn't want to count the holes. Does not want to count to a million. Wants to be as good as he can be.

He shoves the toe of his tennis shoe beneath the short leg of the table. Feels the weight of the table in his toe like a dart. He sits on his right hand to keep his fingers from poking every little hole. To keep from embarrassing Caddie one more time. To keep from being sent away someplace.

When the waitress arrives, Cooper's mother lets him order the pizza. "One large pepperoni pizza with extra cheese," he says.

Caddie rolls her eyes.

"Did you find a bathing suit this time?" their mother asks.

Caddie nods. Reaches for her bag. Holds up a shiny silver bathing suit in two small pieces. "It was on sale."

"Looks nice," their mother says.

"Looks nice," Cooper says.

Caddie rolls her eyes again.

The waitress brings them glasses of water and a pile of napkins.

"I heard Mr. Bell is finally out of the hospital," their mother says.

Poor Mr. Bell. Poor Mr. Bell. Poor Mr. Bell. "I will take him some ice cream," Cooper says.

"That's a nice idea, Cooper," his mother says.

The waitress returns with the giant pizza. Sets it down in the center of the table. "Can I get you anything else?"

"We're good," Caddie says.

"No, thank you," their mother says.

Cooper picks off the pepperoni with his left hand, one by one. Makes a pepperoni tower at the side of his plate.

"Why do you always make us order pepperoni pizza when you won't eat the pepperoni?" Caddie says with lots of mad in her voice. "It doesn't make any sense. Then I have to eat pepperoni pizza and I don't even like it."

"It would be nice if you wouldn't waste it," his mother says.

Cooper wishes he could eat the pepperoni tower. But pepperoni is hot and spicy. Like fire. "Pepperoni pizza is the most popular kind of pizza," he says. "Everybody loves pepperoni."

"Then prove it," Caddie says, picking up a circle

of pepperoni. "And open your mouth."

Cooper looks at Caddie's face. Her beautiful smooth, pink face. And the rubbery piece of pepperoni in her hand.

"It won't hurt you, Coop. Just open your mouth."

The pepperoni comes closer and closer. Cooper shakes his head.

"C'mon, Cooper. Just once. It's not poison. It's not going to kill you."

Kill, kill, kill.

He shakes his head again. His mother looks at him, at Caddie, and looks away, her lips tight like stretched rubber bands. Her tears are ferociously strong. He can see the muscles in his mother's face weaken and pucker. Pepperoni must be very important to her.

"Not today, Caddie," his mother says.

"Why, Mom? If everyone else eats pepperoni, he can too."

His mother shakes her head. Her eyes still glisten.

A girl with fluorescent orange fingernails at the next table watches Caddie. Flings her long blond hair the way Caddie flings hers. Cooper doesn't want to embarrass Caddie one more time. Doesn't want his mother's eyes to shine with tears. Does not want to be sent away. He wants to be like everyone else. Like people who eat pepperoni pizza. Without a care in the world.

"C'mon, Cooper. I dare you."

He shuts his eyes. Squeezes his hands into fists.

For Caddie. Only for Caddie.

He opens his mouth.

The slice of pepperoni lands on his tongue. Spit collects in his cheeks—ready to put out the fire. Saliva pools in his throat. He gags and spits. Caddie pinches his lips shut. "You can do it, Coop. Trust me."

There is no fire. No burn. He is not dying.

It is still true. Everything Caddie says really is getting more and more believable every day.

He chews the pepperoni. Thinks. Thinks of secrets and truths. He will not water the ivy ever again because his mother knows the truth and it will remind her of all the things she cannot bring back to life. He thinks of The Grinner and Caddie's white teeth and sparkling eyes in the night. He thinks of Mike. Mike has a secret. So does Cooper. Secrets are why they are friends. He swallows the pepperoni. Opens his eyes to a living world. His smiling mother. Nothing is on fire. Not even his tongue.

"Look," Caddie says.

A police car turns the corner, drives across the turtle racetrack. Stops in front of DJ's Liquors. And then another police car. And another. "One, two, three," Cooper counts. "Six policemen."

"Must be the whole force," Caddie says.

"Oh, Caddie," their mother says. "It's a small town. Why would they need any more?"

The waitress picks up Caddie's plate. Nods at Cooper's short stack of pepperoni. "Still working on that?"

"It is my life's work," Cooper says. He points across the street. "Is that a sting operation?"

The waitress reaches for his mother's plate. Looks up. "Another robbery, I bet. That'd be the fifth one this summer. Someone got us too. They think it's the same gang."

Sparkling Oz. Flailing turtles. The fireworks. "I bet I know who it is," Cooper says.

"Now, Cooper," his mother says. "Don't get carried away."

"Who?" Caddie says.

"The Loch Ness Monster," he says.

"Oh, Cooper," his mother says.

"You're funny," the waitress says.

"Really?" Caddie says.

Cooper and Caddie have a secret. The secret makes him feel sick to his stomach. "I'm full. Can we go home?" Cooper says.

"What, no ice cream?" His mother pats him on the head.

"I want ice cream," Caddie says.

"If Caddie can eat ice cream, I can eat ice cream," he says because he needs a happy thought. His mother puts her credit card away and they cross the street to The Whole Scoop ice cream stand.

Cooper ties flies when they get home. He ties flies until bedtime. He will finish these flies for Mike and he will never tie flies again. He will tell Mike his fingers hurt. He will tell Mike his mother won't let him. No, he won't. He cannot lie. But he cannot tell the whole truth. He will never tell Mike he feels sorry for the fish. That he wants all fish to be the big one that got away. Mike likes to fish. Mike will not understand.

At midnight, Cooper is too tired to read. Too tired to lay out his rocks. Too tired to write in his notebook. He thinks he might sleep like a log. Like the dead. No, not like the dead. He must unthink that word. *Dead.*

He lies beneath the thin and cool sheet. Awake. Caddie's bed creaks as she rolls over in her sleep. A loon calls with a heart so full of love it shudders. An acorn drops on the roof. Rolls. The loon calls again. On the other side of the cabin, his mother gets up. Goes into the kitchen.

Cooper lies still. Still enough to hear every movement. Every breath. Every thought. He hears the pump. The clink of a glass. He knows his mother has looked at the dead ivy and pricked her heart on its needle-tipped stem.

He watches the moonlit shadows on his walls. Pictures The Father as a giant caddis fly, sputtering across the top of still, dawn-gray water. Thinks of the fish, swimming. Teased. Tricked. Trickery is a tactic of the enemy. He wants to whisper a secret to all the fish: *Do not eat the caddis fly. Even if you fight for your life, you will die. And you will never know what happened.*

Now Cooper is thirsty. He wants a drink. He waits until the house is quiet. Tiptoes to the kitchen. Pumps the water. Sees the ivy in the garbage. Dead. Nothing you can do about it.

It is a truth. Out in the open.

He goes back to his room, to Grandpa's old, safe bedroom, and turns on the light. "It's just me,

Amicus," he whispers before he opens his notebook to a clean page.

Some truths are easier when they aren't secrets anymore.

He leaves the light on and reaches for *Tom Sawyer. He. He. He. Was. Was. Was. Gloomy. Gloomy. Gloomy . . . He was gloomy and desperate.*

Cooper is surprised. Surprised that brave Tom Sawyer is sad. Forsaken and friendless, Tom Sawyer has made up his mind to leave his home and become a pirate. Cooper thinks of Mike. The Mike who looks like Mike but acts like an alien being. For a tiny moment, between the words *aye-aye* and *sir*, Cooper wonders what it would be like to build a raft and sail away.

ILLUSIONS

A magician in a tuxedo and a tall black hat waves a magic wand. It swirls and blurs in the air. Flowers turn into blue pigeons. Suddenly, blue pigeons fly around Cooper's room with a great fluttering of wings. People in the crowd laugh and clap and ooh and ahh.

Like the magician, Cooper waves his arm in the air. Wakes up in the dark. He reaches under his pillow for his flashlight. Turns it on. No pigeons. Just a big gray moth on the wall above his head. Amicus croaks with hunger. A moth is not a happy thought. A blue pigeon flying around his room is. He has dreamed a happy thought.

What day is it?

Cooper climbs out of bed. Stands in front of his calendar with his flashlight. *One, two, three,* he counts. All the way to twelve. Twelve days left at the cabin. He wishes he had a magic wand. With a magic wand, he could slow time and never have to go back to school. Never hear the whispers behind his back. Or speed up time and never have time to worry. Magic would make all the difference in the world. No wonder magicians create illusions. Illusions make people happy.

He opens his dictionary. Finds the words that begin with Il. *Il-lu-pi. Il-luse. Il-lu-sion.* His finger stops on the page. He reads the long definition. Likes this part the most: *A false show. An erroneous perception of reality.* What if he weren't Cooper? What if he could make That Boy go away forever? What if he were an illusion? He writes this down in his notebook:

If I could be an illusion of reality, I would make people happy.

"Amicus," Cooper whispers in the still-dark of the morning, "today I will be an illusion. I will not be what I appear to be. I will appear to be normal." Everything else will be real. Like ice cream. Because you cannot eat illusions.

Ice cream. Today is the day to take Mr. Bell some ice cream.

The cupboards are almost bare. Cooper snaps five graham crackers and a chocolate bar into pieces. Pulls the stem from the strawberries. Mashes the berries to a pulp. Adds two bananas. He pours the last of the sugar into the ice cream maker. Scratches a mosquito bite on his wrist. Scratches the welt until it bleeds.

He washes his hands, and then he adds ice and what is left of the rock salt. Then he turns, and turns and turns the crank. And looks. Turns the crank and looks. *Patience, patience, patience. Scratch, scratch, scratch.* He pumps the water. Washes his hands. Turns the crank and looks.

Caddie finds him in the kitchen. "Cooper, you can't eat ice cream for breakfast."

"I'm not. I'm making ice cream for Mr. Bell."

"What time did you get up?"

All concepts are illusions. They can disappear without warning. Time does not change reality. "Time is an illusion," he says.

"Cooper!"

Cooper is Caddie's illusion of mad. *Don't think. Don't think. Don't think.* "I don't know what time I got up. Do you want to go with me?"

"No." Caddie opens a cupboard and gets out a bowl. Opens another cupboard for the puffed rice cereal. The next cupboard she opens and slams shut. "Where's the sugar?"

The sugar is gone. Used up. Kaput. "In the ice cream," he says, cranking and cranking and cranking.

"COOOO-PER!"

Cooper imagines his name shooting from Caddie's mouth like a burst of flame, landing on the ice shelf. Slicing glaciers like a laser beam. Warming the globe. *No, no, no.* Think a happy thought. Like ice cream. Like glaciers made of strawberries and chocolate bars. Enough to feed the whole world.

He carries the big metal bowl full of ice cream to the road and walks along the crumbled edge of tar. *Déjà vu, déjà vu, déjà vu.* He knows he is small and the world is very, very large. The ice cream bowl burns his hands with cold. Numbs his fingers. He is glad cold is an illusion. Soon the sensation will disappear like magic.

The mosquito bite on his wrist itches. He rubs it against his pants until it bleeds again. Bears can smell blood from three miles away. Bears are not illusions. *Don't think about bears. Don't think about bears. Don't think about bears.* He hurries. Hurries around the bend to the plain white house with green shutters. No misspelled sign. No other man's treasures. The giant black bell is all alone in the yard.

The bell is not an illusion.

What if Mr. Bell is?

Maybe he should go home. No, he can't go home. There is only one destination in the whole very large world for Mr. Bell's ice cream. Cooper stares at the fancy B on Mr. Bell's door. With his elbow, he thumps on the door one, two, three times. A woman with short black hair and a nametag that says "MARY ANN" on her pocket answers the door. Mary Ann is too big and strong to be an illusion. "Yes?" she says.

"Is Mr. Bell home?"

"Is he expecting you?"

Caddie has his mother's sister's book. Cooper has his favorite food. "Yes," he says. "I have his ice cream."

Mary Ann smiles. "He loves ice cream. Follow me."

Cooper follows Mary Ann into a big living room. Mr. Bell sits in a reclined chair, cupped like an astronaut, in front of a window as big as a spaceship's bridge. For a split second, Cooper imagines Mr. Bell as the first man to land on Tezorene. Ever.

A blue plaid blanket covers Mr. Bell from his

knees to his shoulders. Plastic tubes run from his nose to a tank of air that sucks and squirts and breathes. His ancient eyes are closed.

"Mr. Bell," Mary Ann says. "Someone . . ." She looks at Cooper. Waits.

Today Cooper is not Cooper. He is an illusion. "A friend," he says.

"A friend has brought you some ice cream, Mr. Bell."

Mr. Bell opens his eyes. "Hell's bells," he says. "It's you." Long, bony fingers crawl out from under the blanket. Flip a lever. The chair pops Mr. Bell right side up. "Must've fallen asleep." Mr. Bell coughs. "Darn waste of time, sleep is, wouldn't you say?"

Time. Time is an illusion. "Yes," Cooper says. "Especially when there's ice cream." He holds out the bowl.

Mary Ann is not an illusion, but she has disappeared.

"Ice cream?" Mr. Bell peers into the metal bowl in Cooper's cold hands. "Mary Ann!" Mr. Bell's voice is gruff and crackly. "Can you bring us two spoons?"

Mary Ann brings two spoons. "Pull up a stool," Mr. Bell says. Cooper puts the bowl in Mr. Bell's lap, pulls up a stool. Its seat is the shape of a duck. No. A loon. Mr. Bell pushes at the tubes across his chest. "Nothing better than ice cream for breakfast, wouldn't you say?"

Cooper wants his own bowl. He doesn't want Mr. Bell's spit on his spoon. In his ice cream. Germs are not an illusion. They are invisible. There is a difference. *Don't think about germs. Don't think about germs. Don't think about germs.*

Mr. Bell holds up the bowl. His arms shake. "You go first. You're my guest."

Cooper is glad to go first. He dips his spoon. Digs out a bit of candy bar. Mr. Bell dips his spoon next. Purses his wrinkled lips around the bite of ice cream. "Strawberry?"

Cooper nods. Mr. Bell smiles. Cooper chews a chunk of cold graham cracker. Mr. Bell sucks on his next bite. The oxygen tank hisses.

"Strawberry," Mr. Bell says slowly. "And banana?" He works his tongue around and around. "And chocolate?" He swallows. "So, what do you call this kind of ice cream?"

Names. Names never go away. Not even if you die. Names are not illusions. "It doesn't have a name yet," Cooper says.

"Cooper, right?"

"What?" Cooper says.

"Your name. It's Cooper, right?" Mr. Bell coughs. Cooper nods. "Then we'll call it Cooper's Crazy Quilt ice cream," Mr. Bell says.

"Why?"

"Because my mother used to make quilts from scraps of old fabric. A little bit of everything. Called them crazy quilts." Mr. Bell coughs. Cooper imagines wet ice cream in Mr. Bell's lungs. Clogged. Clogged like a drain with the last bit of soap lodged in its trap. He moves the bowl.

Cooper suddenly has a cold headache. He stops eating. Moves the bowl back to Mr. Bell's lap. Looks around the room. Masks that appear to be enormous caddis flies hang on one wall. Photographs cover the far wall in perfect rows like diplomas. Like a hundred diplomas. "Are you a photographer?" Cooper says. The question sounds dumb to Cooper. He wants to write this down, but he is sitting on his notebook.

Sometimes polite questions are dumb questions.

"Took pictures my whole life. Most of it anyway. Ninety-seven last April. Damn near a hundred years. My God. That's a lot of sunrises."

Cooper can believe it. Mr. Bell is the oldest living

person he has ever known. Cooper taps his fingers. Calculates. "At least thirty-five thousand four hundred and five."

"What?" Mr. Bell says. His mouth is full of ice cream. Ice cream strings hang from his upper lip like thin stalactites.

"Sunrises," Cooper says. "But the precise answer depends on your birthdate."

"Feels like more." Mr. Bell laughs and swallows at the same time. Coughs. Almost chokes. His slimy white tongue waves in his open, quivering mouth. Ice cream runs in the rivulets above his crinkled lip. "You're a smart kid, aren't you?"

Smart is an illusion. Cooper isn't sure about old. Wrinkles and white hair are not illusions. But you grow old over time. And time is an illusion. Therefore, perhaps, old is an illusion. "How did you get to be so old, Mr. Bell?"

"The same way you got to be so smart. It's in the genes. Not much you can do about it. Everything else I did on purpose."

Cooper looks back at the wall of pictures. "Like climbing Machu Picchu?"

Mr. Bell swivels slowly in his chair. "You know about Machu Picchu?"

Cooper nods. "I've read about the ancient Incan landmark in books."

"Never was much for reading," Mr. Bell says. He turns back to the bowl of ice cream in his lap.

"You can learn a lot by reading," Cooper says.

"Maybe," Mr. Bell says. "But where's the thrill?"

"What thrill?" Cooper says.

"The thrill of doing it." Mr. Bell holds his spoon tight in his fist. Waves it in the air. "The thrill of surviving so you can tell the world all about it." Mr. Bell coughs.

Cooper shivers inside. "But what if you don't survive?"

Mr. Bell snorts. "If I'd looked at it that way, I might never have done anything."

"Did you tell the world all about it?"

"You bet I did!" Mr. Bell nods toward the photographs. "You know what they say. A picture paints a thousand words."

Cooper has never heard anyone say that. He digs out a chunk of banana at the edge of the bowl. Slides off his stool with his spoon in his hand, walks around a coffee table made of shiny yellow metal, and walks closer to the wall of photos. He zeroes in on a raft of people riding the rapids in a river. "Where is that?"

"Alaska."

Wolves and grizzly bears and giant mosquitoes and moose live in the Land of the Midnight Sun. They are not illusions. They are real. "Were you scared?"

"Hell, yes. We trekked in. But I told myself people had been doing it for hundreds of years. Told myself the same thing when I climbed Everest. Besides, it was the plane ride that damn near scared the . . ." Mr. Bell laughs. Shakes his head like he can't believe it. "I guess you're right. Maybe I'm not supposed to be here. Been defying the odds my whole life."

Maybe it is possible. If Mr. Bell should not be here, maybe he is an illusion.

Cooper walks the length of the wall, staring at the pictures. He wants to count them. Touch their sharp corners. He wants to straighten the picture of the people in the raft, water around their heads like white lace, but the picture does not belong to him. He should not touch it. He will not touch it. Today he is an illusion. Today he is normal. He will be polite. He clasps the spoon in one hand, puts the other hand in his pocket.

"What's the scariest thing you ever did?"

"Got a picture of it right there." Mr. Bell points his spoon at the wall. "You tell me."

Cooper scrutinizes the pictures one by one. A man and a woman all dressed up and getting married. Mount Rushmore, eye-to-eye with Abe Lincoln, someone's feet dangling from a helicopter. "Are those your feet?" Cooper turns back to Mr. Bell. Mr. Bell nods.

Cooper keeps going. John F. Kennedy, the 35th president. The Taj Mahal. Muhammed Ali with a big gloved hand over his head. The Champ. More presidents. More famous people. A helicopter on fire in a jungle. More famous places. A close-up of a mountain climber, his face covered in frost. German soldiers stacking cement blocks, making a wall taller than they are. Lou Gehrig leaning on a baseball bat. Cooper pauses. Lou Gehrig was his grandfather's hero. "The Iron Horse," he says.

"Smart boy," Mr. Bell says.

But Lou Gehrig was not an iron horse. Not really.

Cooper backs up. Remembers what Mr. Bell said about climbing Mount Everest. Looks at the mountain climber. Clouds above his head. Nothing but icy-blue sky at his feet. The mountain climber is suspended in thin air. "That one," he says, and he knows he's right. "Climbing Mount Everest is the scariest thing you ever did." He turns toward Mr. Bell. Waits.

"Good guess. Plenty scary, all right, to hang by a thread from a mountainside. But you're wrong," Mr. Bell says with his mouth full. And then he swallows. And licks his lips.

Cooper is confused. He feels like he's playing a game that is not a game.

"I'll give you a clue," Mr. Bell says. "It's the only picture up there I didn't take myself."

Cooper looks back at the wall of pictures. "That could be all of them," Cooper says.

Mr. Bell's lips push together. Protrude. "You got me there," he says. And then Mr. Bell wipes his mouth with the fringe of the blue blanket. "But the truth is, there's only one picture of me in this whole darn place." Mr. Bell laughs and coughs again. "The first one, top left." He waves his spoon in the air. "My wedding picture."

Cooper looks at the photograph of the man and woman more closely. Sees their happy smiles. Can't find Mr. Bell anywhere in the man's smooth face and tall body. He wants to begin his sentence with "I believe," but he hears Caddie's voice. *No one says "I believe."* "You tricked me," Cooper says.

"Not at all," Mr. Bell laughs. "Getting married is the scariest thing I've ever done." Mr. Bell pokes at the ice cream with his spoon. Stops. "Best thing too." Mr. Bell stares out the big window. Stares and stares. The oxygen tank hisses and squirts in the silence. The silence that isn't silent at all.

Cooper knows Mr. Bell sees a memory in the window. "Excuse me, Mr. Bell," he says. He pulls out his notebook. Flips open the cover. "I don't want to forget something." And then he writes,

> Sometimes the scariest things you do are the best things you do.

"You look like a reporter," Mr. Bell says. He coughs. Pokes again at the ice cream. "What's the scoop?"

"Scoop?" Cooper says.

"What are you writing?"

No one has ever asked Cooper what he is writing. No one has ever read his words. But Cooper feels like he is in school. Like Mr. Bell is the teacher. He knows he must answer this question. He feels a shiver in his breath as he reads his words out loud: "Sometimes the scariest things you do are the best things you do."

Mr. Bell nods. "That's true. But I bet nothing scares

you. You're too smart. Just like your grandfather."

Mr. Bell does not know Cooper's secrets or his truths. He doesn't know about That Boy. And he doesn't know about the things that scare him. Like The Father. The Grinner. And fireworks. And fire. Mr. Bell knows only the good things. He knows about ice cream. And Grandpa.

Cooper pictures his grandfather under water. Dead. Nothing you can do about it.

But what if there is? What if there is something he can do about it?

What if there is something you can do about everything?

"I am afraid of some things," Cooper says.

"Like what?"

All Cooper can think of is water. The lake. His grandfather. Cooper wants to wash. Wants to stomp his leg, but Mr. Bell would want him to go away and he doesn't want to go away. He looks to the window. To Mr. Bell's memory window, and writes this down against the palm of his hand:

Memories can be illusions if the truth is too hard to bear.

He wishes he had a memory window. He wants to remember something else. Something besides Grandpa's desperate eyes. He wants a different picture in his mind. One that paints a thousand happy words.

Mr. Bell is still watching him. Waiting for an answer.

"Like water," Cooper finally says.

Mr. Bell nods again. "Me too. Anyone in his right mind should be afraid of water."

Cooper likes this room that looks over the tree-tops at the world. The room hisses with life. His own breath hisses too. His mind shuffles Mr. Bell's pictures and Mr. Bell's words and his own fear. That Boy is standing at the ready. Cooper points at the photograph of the raft. "Then how did you do that?"

"Easy," Mr. Bell says. "Logic, preparation, and caution. It's how I ever did anything. Living and dying." Mr. Bell laughs. Sucks on his teeth. "Except get married. Some things you just do without thinking." He waves his spoon in the air. "And I'd give everything for a chance to do it all over again."

"Even the raft?"

"Especially the raft." Mr. Bell makes a funny face at the silver mixing bowl. "Look at that. I ate the whole damn thing." He laughs. Stops. Looks out his window for many quiet seconds. "And if I were younger, I'd take you with me."

Cooper thinks of swimming and getting water up his nose. He remembers flippers and goggles. There was a time when he wasn't afraid, but that was a very long time ago. He shakes his head. "I'm not a very good swimmer," he says. "I might drown."

"Then you have to learn how to swim. That's called preparation." Mr. Bell clears his throat. "Here's a question for you." Mr. Bell coughs. Coughs and coughs. Coughs until Mary Ann appears. She fiddles with the tubes in Mr. Bell's nose. He waves her away. "Exactly . . ." Mr. Bell clears his throat again. His voice is soft and whispery. "Exactly how many people do you know who have drowned?"

Grandpa had a heart attack. He did not drown. *Did not drown. Did not drown. Did not drown.* "Exactly zero," Cooper says.

"See?" Mr. Bell pats the loon stool, slowly, as if his hand weighs a hundred pounds. "That's where the logic comes in." He stares out the big window.

Cooper sits back down. Looks where Mr. Bell looks. Suddenly, a big bird with a white head and brown wings a mile wide swoops above the trees. "I think it's an eagle," Cooper says.

"It is," Mr. Bell says in a whisper as if the eagle might hear him. He takes a deep breath. "Mary Ann! Where's Betsy?" And then he winks—a slow sticky wink. "Betsy's my best gal."

Mr. Bell is quiet. The eagle soars from view.

"Damn."

"What's the best picture you ever took?" Cooper asks.

Mr. Bell stares at Cooper. For a long, scary moment Cooper is certain Mr. Bell's milky eyes have stopped working. "The best picture is right here." Mr. Bell taps his temple with his long forefinger. His wrinkled lips lift upward into a smile. "The photographs just help me remember." Mr. Bell sighs. Breathes. Coughs.

Mary Ann reappears with Betsy in her hands. Betsy is not a gal. She is an old camera.

"For a second there I thought we'd left her at the hospital," Mary Ann says.

Betsy is too heavy for Mr. Bell. His bony hands shake. "Stay right here, Mary Ann." He rests his elbow on the arm of his chair. Points the long camera lens at the lake. Waits. Waits and waits. The eagle flies near the shore. Rises. Floats above the trees. Mr. Bell clicks the shutter. "Got 'im." He adjusts the knobs. "Now you get one of us." He hands the camera to Mary Ann. "And you stand right here by me, my boy." Mr. Bell reaches for Cooper. Puts his hand on Cooper's shoulder.

My boy.

Mr. Bell said, "My boy," just like Grandpa.

Up close, Mr. Bell smells like Swiss cheese. Cooper wants to plug his nose. Wants to duck under Mr. Bell's arm and run. Knows running would be mean. Cooper breathes through his mouth. Feels his shoulder grow warm. A hundred years' worth of warm. He takes a deep breath. Forgets to breathe through his mouth. Smells Swiss cheese again. And soap. And something else.

Cooper inhales through his nose. Thinks. Shuffles the memories. Remembers.

He smells *old age.*

And maybe his grandfather's boat.

No, not just the boat. He smells his grandfather. *My boy.* He inhales again. Thinks he might burst. Burst with memories. He puts his arm on the back of Mr. Bell's chair. Moves it to his bony shoulder. Feels Mr. Bell's clavicle. He smiles for the camera. Hears the shutter click. The camera is old and the picture is an illusion.

But Cooper's smile is not.

SURPRISES

Cooper walks home, facing traffic, a small particle of alien life on the road. He follows the line between the tar and the grass. Mary Ann washed and dried the big steel mixing bowl. Empty and warm, it makes a good helmet. He is a Tezornaut.

He wonders about this strange place, Earth. He can walk here without his thermomatic protection. His arms and legs have not turned to liquid in the singular solar heat.

Perhaps Earth contains a knowledge he will take home to his people. If he can rebuild his spaceship, he will transport cool air to Tezorene. Winds and breezes and also the odd liquid that mostly flows south, but does occasionally flow north, and sometimes accumulates in large, subterranean vessels. The invisible liquid is called water. It sucks humans to death. *No, no, no.* Not just death. It gives life too. Humans also use it for what they call "recreation."

A distant motor.

A car.

Cooper makes perfect, careful steps, one behind the other at the edge of the road. The car passes him. Another car goes by. And then a white Jeep. A white Jeep with leaping fish painted on its door. The Jeep slows. Stops. Backs up. The window slides down. "Hey, Cooper! Is that you?"

Cooper looks inside the Jeep. Spies the Earthling known as Mike. When he nods, the steel bowl slips over his eyes.

"Why do you have a mixing bowl on your head?"

"Meep," Cooper says in Tezorinian. He cups his hand in greeting—the way the Tezornauts do. "Nice to observe your sudden appearance. Surprises are quite typical of life on this planet."

"Meep," Mike says. "Can I give you a lift to your space station?"

"Meep," Cooper says and gets into the Jeep.

"I haven't seen you in ages. Not since you quit working for me."

Cooper pictures Jack's big fish as it lay dying. Sees its glistening eye. "Meep," he says in a very low voice.

"Did you finish *Tom Sawyer*?"

"Meep," Cooper says in an even lower tone that means no.

"Cooper, this humanoid requests to speak in the language of its own people. Communication will be a lot easier."

"Meep, meep," Cooper says. "Request granted." He removes his Tezornaut helmet.

"How's your summer going?" Mike asks. "I can't believe it's almost over."

"We will be here exactly twelve more days."

"I know I promised to take you fishing. But we've been so busy at the shop." Mike looks in his rearview mirror. Cooper looks too. Nothing is behind them. "How's Caddie?" Mike asks.

Caddie is mad because Cooper used all the sugar to make ice cream for Mr. Bell. And she's mad because there is nothing to do at the cabin except play games and lie in the sun. "She is bored silly," Cooper says.

Mike frowns. "There's a new mini-golf course that finally opened up on the highway. Blackbeard's Bounty. That could be fun."

Blackbeard was a pirate. Like Tom Sawyer. Cooper would like to be a pirate and play miniature golf with Mike and never have to go fishing or get on a raft. "Okay," Cooper says. "Let's go."

"What?" Mike says. "You and me?" Mike looks at his watch. "Uh . . ." Mike is making a big decision. "I . . . uh . . ." They pass the red mailbox. "Shoot. That was your driveway, wasn't it?"

Cooper looks over his shoulder, watches the red mailbox disappear behind a tree. "It's the red one that says 'Mills.'"

Mike pulls into the next driveway. Stops. Pine trees block his view. He looks in the rearview mirror. Backs out. Slams on the brakes. Cooper lunges forward. The metal bowl falls to the floor. The Jake's Plumbing truck has come out of nowhere. Jake honks its horn.

"Sorry," Mike says as if Jake can hear him. He turns the Jeep around. Finds the red mailbox.

"Do you think it is truly possible?" Cooper asks.

"What?" Mike says.

"To play mini-golf."

"Now?"

Cooper knows Mike does not want to play mini-golf right now. Would like to say "meep" in the lowest possible tone. "I can't, Cooper. I have to get to work. Maybe some other time."

"Meep," Cooper says.

When they roll down the driveway, Cooper's mother is tying a string around the stalks of her tomato plants. Caddie comes out the door in her bathing suit and a towel wrapped around her waist. She looks like a hula dancer. Her nose is bright red with sunburn.

Caddie and his mother stare at the Jeep like confused Earthlings. As if the Jeep is from outer space. Cooper waves through the windshield, grabs his Tezornaut helmet, and jumps to the ground. Mike gets out too.

"I was beginning to worry about you," his mother says.

"No need to worry when I'm with Mike," Cooper says. He hands his mother the big mixing bowl. "Mr. Bell ate almost all the ice cream by himself."

"Yeah, right," Caddie says.

Cooper's mother smiles a smile as big as an eagle's wingspan. Not that big really, but Cooper thinks of something really big because he has not seen her smile in a really long time.

Mike says hi.

Caddie says hi. And then she says, "How's life at the bait shop?"

Mike rocks from foot to foot. "Good," he says. His face turns as red as the strawberries in Mr. Bell's ice cream and his pimples disappear. "The fish are biting like crazy."

"Cool," Caddie says.

"Yeah," Mike says.

Cooper wishes he were a real Tezornaut. He would like to abduct Mike and take him to his planet. Save Mike from this embarrassing Earthling moment he has read about in Caddie's magazines. "Come in my room, Mike. I want to show you something."

"Can't. I really have to get going."

"It will only take a second," Cooper says, but he knows it will take longer. "I mean two minutes."

Caddie smiles.

"Okay," Mike says.

Mike follows Cooper to his room. Cooper points at the aquarium. "That's my frog. His name is Amicus the Great." Cooper is glad to show Mike his frog. Glad to have a real friend at the cabin. "You can feed him if you want."

"Amicus, huh?"

"Yeah," Cooper says. "*Amicus* means 'friend' in Latin."

Mike bends down, eye-to-eye with Amicus.

"He's a green frog," Mike says. "You know what that means." Mike pops a food nugget into his palm. "He'd rather be in a lake and eat real flies."

"He's not ready yet," Cooper says.

Mike drops the food nugget into the water. Amicus snaps it up. "Just imagine if you were cooped up in there with people staring at you all the time," Mike says.

"Just imagine if you had to do something for the first time. And you had to do it all alone. And you had no idea how to do it."

"You have a point there," Mike says.

"Besides, he's my best friend," Cooper says. "Except for you."

"What? Oh. Sure. That's different then." And then Mike says, "I have to go. I'll be late for work."

Cooper walks outside with Mike. The screen door squeaks and snaps shut. Caddie is sitting on the step. "Mike says there's a new mini-golf course called Blackbeard's Bounty. Maybe we could go there sometime."

"I've been by it," his mother says. "It's up on the highway."

"Sounds fun," Caddie says.

"Really?" Mike says. "Maybe you'd like to go

with me." His face turns splotchy red again.

"Now?" Caddie says.

"Uh . . . sure," Mike says. "I guess. I mean . . . yeah. That would be great."

"I thought you had to work," Cooper says.

Mike shrugs. "I can go in later," he says. "My dad won't mind."

"Oh," Cooper says. "Oh," he says again as he feels a tremble in his legs. In his arms. A tremble that makes him want to touch. Want to count. He does not understand Mike. He does not understand friends. "I will read *Tom Sawyer* while you are gone," Cooper says. "The good and famous book you gave me." He puts his hand on the doorknob. The screen door squeaks open.

"Wait a minute, Coop," Caddie says. "If you're not going, I'm not going."

The screen door snaps shut.

"Really?" Cooper says.

Caddie nods. "Just let me get changed."

In an instant, Cooper's mother goes into the house and comes out with her purse. She hands Cooper a twenty-dollar bill. The twenty is crisp and new. He folds it into a perfect square. When Caddie comes outside in her pink T-shirt and white shorts, Cooper whispers to her, "I promise I will not embarrass you." And then he opens the car door for her. "My lady," he says.

"Cooper," she says with mad inching into her voice.

Mike keeps his eyes on the road. No one talks the whole way. A police car passes them on the highway. Mike looks at his speedometer. Slows down. In the silence, Cooper hears a helicopter *thup-thup-thup* above them. He puts his face to the window. Watches the helicopter tilt forward and lift into the sky.

"Look," Cooper says. "A helicopter."

Mike leans close to his windshield. Looks up. "Huh," he says. "They must be giving rides today."

Cooper shudders. He thinks of Mr. Bell in a helicopter, taking a picture of Mount Rushmore. Of Mr. Bell's other picture, the helicopter burning in the jungle. He cannot see the point of riding in a helicopter for fun.

Finally, they arrive at Blackbeard's Bounty—a mountain of a golf course with waterfalls and wrecks of pirate ships glued to the mountainside. Pirate flags mark every hole. "If I were an alien being," Cooper says, "I would take pictures of this great landmark and beam them home to my people."

"Meep, meep," Mike says with a really high voice. Caddie laughs.

Suddenly, another laugh. An unexpected laugh. Cooper's own laugh. He has landed on an alien planet and the people understand what he is trying to say. Smiling, Cooper gets out of the Jeep.

They pick out putters and different colored golf balls at Blackbeard's Souvenir and Snack Shack. "Girls first," Mike says at the first green.

Caddie tees off first. She is the only girl. With a hard smack, her yellow ball ricochets from wall to wall. Rolls through a slit in the ship's wheel—straight for the hole. The ball bounces in and then out of the hole and rolls. Rolls and rolls, down the hill, rolling and rolling until it rolls into a corner and stops. "Wow," Mike says. "Amazing shot."

Mike is making a joke. A joke just for Caddie.

At the waterfall, Cooper lies down on the green. Lays his golf club in front of him like an arrow. Lines up his shot like a pro. He measures the distance with his footsteps. Eyes the angle. Moves the club four millimeters. No. Five millimeters is better. Cooper gets a hole in one.

"Wow," Mike says, and Cooper knows this time Mike really means it.

They take turns teeing off and putting, up and down the pirate mountainside. Caddie laughs every time she hits the ball. She really is having fun. Cooper can see this truth.

The treasure chest on the eighteenth hole opens and closes every six seconds. Caddie looks at her ball. At the treasure chest. Watches the treasure chest open and close. Looks at her ball. She swings and smacks the ball. It bounces off the top of the closed chest, misses a tree, bounces past a little girl standing nearby with a million braids in her hair for a hole in one on green 15—three holes away. The little girl watches the ball and laughs. Caddie laughs so hard she snorts. Cooper laughs too. Mike laughs so hard he has to sit down on a bench. "I can't breathe," he says.

Cooper stops laughing. What was he thinking? He cannot forget his responsibilities. He watches Mike closely. Mike is breathing. Mike is not dying. Mike is exaggerating.

Cooper adds up the scores. Caddie has ninety-two points. Cooper has seventy-nine points. Mike has sixty-eight points. "You win, Mike."

"I've played it before," Mike says. Then he slaps Cooper on the back like a good friend. "You played a good game."

"What about me?" Caddie says. She starts laughing all over again.

Cooper has just figured something out. He pulls his notebook from his pocket.

Making stupid jokes and laughing a lot means you might be falling in love.

"You?" Mike says. "I'm going to have to give you lessons."

Caddie giggles.

"Private lessons?" Cooper says.

"Cooper," Caddie says. "What have I told you?" Her face turns red again. "You have to mind your own business."

Cooper turns around. Writes this down:

If everyone minded their own business, the world would be a very lonely place.

They turn in their clubs at Blackbeard's Souvenir and Snack Shack. "That was fun," Caddie says.

"Maybe we should play again before you go home," Mike says.

"That would be great," Cooper says.

"Maybe," Caddie says.

"Look," Cooper says. He points at the shelves of souvenirs. Points at a flag that reads "Blackbeard's Bounty." Thinks of Tom and Huck playing pirates. "Is there money left over?"

Caddie shakes her head. "Just a few dollars. Not enough."

"I've got it," Mike says. "One Jolly Roger," he says to the clerk.

Cooper does not want the Jolly Roger flag. Does not like the skull and crossbones. A flag of death. He doesn't say anything. He must be polite. The flag is a gift from Mike.

Mike waves the flag as he hands it to Cooper. "Argh," he says.

"Argh," Cooper says. He holds the flag very, very still.

From the corner of his eye, Cooper sees someone running. A boy. A boy running with long legs—like a frog. Running across the highway. Running into the parking lot of Blackbeard's Bounty. He sees his blond hair bouncing. Knows who it is before he sees his grin.

"Hey, man!" The Grinner yells. Mike looks up.

Cooper freezes. He wishes his spaceship could

lift off with Caddie and Mike on board. He reaches for Caddie's hand, so she won't be left behind. Mike looks at them with startled eyes. Looks back at The Grinner.

"I thought I saw your Jeep. Finally got your license. Cool." The Grinner is out of breath. "Hey, I wondered . . ." The Grinner looks over his shoulder. Up and down the highway. His long blond hair twists and falls on his shoulders. The Grinner puts his arm around Mike. Pulls him toward the parking lot, away from Cooper and Caddie. "Could you spot me some money?" The Grinner says.

Mike opens his wallet. "How much?"

"Like maybe a couple hundred?"

"Dollars? Are you crazy? I don't carry that kind of money."

The Grinner whispers. Cooper hears the word "vacation." Mike looks at Caddie. At Cooper. Holds up one finger. "Just a sec."

Tall Boy and The Grinner. Together again. They walk across the parking lot. Get into Mike's Jeep. Shut the doors.

Something isn't right. Something is wrong. Very wrong. Cooper stomps his leg one, two, three . . .

"Cooper, don't," Caddie says. "We have enough

money left for ice cream. I'll buy you some ice cream. Just don't do that."

Cooper isn't hungry. But That Boy is. That Boy is hungry to run. Hungry to touch. But Cooper can't run. He can't leave Caddie alone. Not by herself. "Okay," he says. He doesn't want to embarrass Caddie one more time, but he can't help it. Mike is with The Grinner. *Can't help it. Can't help it. Can't help it.* That Boy pulls Cooper's hands into the air. He reaches for water. The clean everlasting water.

"Just don't do that, Cooper. Sit down. I'll be right back."

Cooper sits down on a wooden bench. With Tezornaut vision, he can see beyond the souvenir shack to the road. Can see the police cars—one, two, three, four, silent, like prowling cats—roll into the parking lot. He reaches into the air. Reaches and washes. Scrubs and scrubs.

Caddie comes back. "Don't, Cooper, please. Here. It's an ice cream sandwich. It's all they had. Please, Cooper." Caddie peels the wrapper. Grabs his right hand. Puts the ice cream sandwich in his fingers. "Eat it, Coop. Please. Everyone is looking at us."

Cooper shakes his head.

"Yes, Cooper," Caddie says with desperate eyes. "Just eat it."

Cooper takes a bite of the ice cream sandwich. Knows Caddie is looking in the wrong direction. Over her shoulder, Cooper watches the policemen get out of their cars. Sees the tall policeman in a lime-green vest draw his gun. "Caddie," he whispers.

"What?" she says. When he points, she looks in the right direction.

Cooper imagines his throat like a drain. Imagines all the ice cream he has ever eaten in his whole life. Clogged. He feels the oxygen sucked out of the air. The crowd closing in like deep water. He cannot breathe.

The police officers circle Mike's white Jeep. One holds a megaphone. "Get out of the car! Keep your hands up and get out of the car. Now!" The powerful voice barrels through the universe.

Caddie squeaks like a million fretting mice. She squeezes Cooper's hand.

One, two, three, four, five, six, seven, eight policemen surround Mike's Jeep. The leaping fish is caught in the net. Can't get away. Nothing you can do about it. Arms point guns like spokes in a bicycle wheel. "I repeat, keep your hands up and get out of the car."

Cooper's muscles clench from the inside out. He tries, but he cannot keep his swallowed food a secret. He heaves and coughs. Ice cream splats to the ground. Spit strings dangle and drip. The crowd steps back. "Oh, Cooper," Caddie says. She takes what's left of the ice cream sandwich. "I'll get you a napkin."

The Jeep doors push open. Two policemen grab The Grinner. Two grab Mike. Spin them around. Flatten them against the Jeep. Mike's eyes are bigger and whiter than Caddie's the night of the fireworks. Whiter than milk.

Overhead, the sound of the helicopter. *Thup, thup, thup.*

But Mike is not the foe.

Cooper thinks of Jack's dead fish. The racing turtles. The minnows, the worms, and the lobsters. All things trapped and scared. Mike is in danger and he can't get away. Cooper wishes he had his cape. His helmet. This time he cannot do nothing. He must save his friend Mike.

"No!" he yells. "No!" Cooper charges for Mike's Jeep. Charges for the policeman with his hand on Mike's shoulder. Grabs the arm with the gun. "Mike is not the foe!" he yells.

Cooper's feet lift from the ground. A gunshot.

A crack in the sky. Cooper hears the gasp of the crowd—the air of the universe escaping. Feels the thunder in his chest. The gravel in his cheek. A burn beneath his eye. His arm twisted behind his back.

From the ground, he can see Caddie's pink T-shirt. She pushes through the crowd with a paper napkin. A white flag. "No!" she screams. "You don't understand." The napkin floats to the ground. Brushes Cooper's nose. Lands next to the Jolly Roger lying on the ground. Cooper sees Caddie upside down. He cannot wash. Cannot stomp his leg. Cannot embarrass her one more time.

"What's your name?" the policeman shouts in Cooper's ear. The policeman pats his pockets. His legs. "What are you doing here?"

The spaceship has crashed into a million pieces. A short in the system. No way to reach his people. No way for his people to reach him. A whisper floats from Cooper's mouth. "Meep."

The policeman stands Cooper on his feet. Cooper wants to run. Wants to count. His hands are bound behind his back. Caddie is crying. He looks down. He knows he has embarrassed her one more time.

Car doors slam. Three police cars roll away. Mike has disappeared.

Caddie whispers, explains. Whispers and cries. Picks up the Jolly Roger flag. Covers her face with her hands.

The officer walks Cooper toward the police car. His partner opens the driver's door. Talks on the radio. Nods. The policeman releases Cooper's handcuffs. When his partner opens the back door of the police car, Caddie hands Cooper the Jolly Roger.

Caddie rides next to Cooper. Behind the black gate. She holds his hand. Stares out the window. Cooper stares at Caddie's kneecap. He can't see over the bump in his cheek. The flag of death is tight in his hand.

Meep, meep, meep.

No one says anything. Not one word down the highway. Not one word the whole way around the lake. Not until the policeman says, "Here?" and Caddie says, "No, the next one. The red one that says 'Mills.'"

Cooper's mother stands up from her garden in slow motion. Weeds in her hand. She stands small beneath the giant Norway pines. Puts her fingertips to her lips.

One policeman opens Caddie's door. The other

policeman opens Cooper's door. Caddie tugs Cooper's hand, lets it go. "C'mon, Coop. We're home."

Their mother trembles. The weeds drop from her hand. "Caddie, what happened?"

Caddie opens her mouth. Nothing comes out.

His mother looks from Caddie to Cooper to the policemen in slow motion. Cooper's heart pounds. His face throbs. His mother puts her arms around him.

"Yes, officer," his mother says.

She doesn't understand it. She can't believe it. She is surprised at Cooper.

"No, officer."

She is sorry. So sorry. Someone could have been killed.

Killed. Killed. Killed.

Killed. Dead. Nothing you can do it about it.

Cooper cannot escape that word.

The police car drives away.

"I'll have to call Dad," his mother says.

Surprises come out of nowhere. Like a fly swatter. Splat.

And nothing is ever the same.

HEROES

"I'm never going on another date as long as I live," Caddie says. Her stomps into the cabin are louder than the squeak of the door. "I'm going to be a spinster and take up knitting."

Cooper runs to his room. Does not mean to slam the door. He is sick to his stomach. He knows he will never eat another ice cream sandwich as long as he lives.

Lives, lives, lives.

Dies, dies, dies.

Gone, gone, gone.

He rolls up the Jolly Roger flag and puts it under his bed. There is nothing jolly about it.

He wants it far away. But he cannot throw it away. It is a gift from his friend, Mike. He must keep it as a reminder. He has tried to save Mike and he has failed.

Someone could have been killed.

Now he must work harder than ever. Work to protect the people he loves. Work to be good. Work extra, extra, extra hard to be normal.

Cooper feels like the innocent bad guy on TV. Nobody understands. Nobody knows the truth. He wishes he could change the channel. Wants to push the remote control. Find the show where he is the hero. Heroes never die, but they can be killed. *Killed, killed, killed.* There is a difference.

He taps on Amicus's aquarium. Amicus lifts his head. Cooper gives him a food nugget. "You are a good, brave boy. Braver than you know."

Cooper lays out his rocks on his bed, one by one: one the size of his fist, two smaller ones, and the tiny one, flat, like a nickel. He misses the biggest rock of all. The grandfather rock. He touches the rocks one by one. Touches them again. And again. Three times three. And writes in his notebook,

Sometimes it is dangerous to be brave.

Cooper grabs *The Adventures of Tom Sawyer* and reads. Reads and reads.

He reads until the sun hangs low in the sky.

Reads so the world does not catch fire and burn.

Tom Sawyer and his pirates go swimming. They smoke pipes. Pretend to be dead.

Sometimes dead is better than alive.

The pirates hide from the townspeople and go to their own funeral. *Hide, hide, hide.* Tom and Huck find buried treasure. Old Muff Potter is innocent. Becky cries. *He's gone now. He's gone now. He's gone now. I'll. I'll. I'll. Never. Never. Never. See. See. See . . . I'll never see him anymore.* Becky is sad that Tom Sawyer is dead. Cooper scratches out his words.

~~Sometimes dead is better than alive.~~
No. Dead is not better than alive.
Not for the people who love you.

Cooper thinks of Grandpa, Mike, and Mr. Bell. Mr. Bell is dying. Mike has been taken away. Cooper feels how Becky feels. Full of grief for someone he will never see again. The funeral in *Tom Sawyer* is supposed to be funny. Like a practical joke.

Practical jokes are oxymorons.

He thinks of caddis flies and pretend fishing. He knows the police were not an illusion. They were not a joke. They were not kidding.

He does not answer the knock on his door.

"Cooper," his mother says softly.

"I am sleeping," he says. Now he must sleep to avoid the lie. He closes his eyes. He cannot sleep. His nerves are on fire.

Cooper reads through the ring of the telephone and the sound of low voices. Through the bray of the pump and dishes clanking. He reads until Caddie goes to bed. His mother too. He reads until the cabin is dark and silent. Reads until everyone knows that Tom and Huck are still alive. He reads until Tom and Becky are lost in the cave. Becky is hungry. And no one can find them.

He cannot sleep.

Cannot stop thinking.

He cannot stop thinking the boathouse is like a cave. A cave dug into the earth on the edge of the water. Cannot stop thinking about what Mr. Bell said. *Logic, preparation, and caution.*

Cooper gets out of bed.

First, he gives Amicus an extra food nugget. Then he packs his backpack with a flashlight, *The*

Adventures of Tom Sawyer, his notebook, a pencil, and his pillow. He tiptoes to the kitchen. Packs graham crackers and juice boxes so he will not be hungry or thirsty like Becky. Takes the keys with the leaping trout keychain, the one with PM, for Patrick Mills, for Grandpa, from its hook in the kitchen. The keychain no one has touched in two years. He folds the checkered brown fishing blanket under his arm. Tiptoes across the cabin. Does not let the screen door slam. Or even squeak.

Fireflies pop and glow in the tall grass. A breeze rustles the oak leaves. Tiny waves brush the shore. *Lap, lap, lap.* They echo like whispers. The sky is clear and dashed with stars. Sagittarius the Archer stands guard. Moonlight shines through the tall Norway pines. Shines on the lake. Still and smooth. The moonbeam guides Cooper to the edge of the water. To the boathouse. To Grandpa's fishing boat. Dark and underground. Like a grave.

No, not a grave. Not a grave. Not a grave. Like the cave in *Tom Sawyer. Cave, cave, cave.*

Cooper puts the key in the lock. Smells the boat before he opens the door. Smells the bitterness of old rubber tires. Damp wood. The cold, wet sand. Sweet pipe tobacco. The door creaks. Sticks in the sand. It will not budge another inch.

Cooper pushes his backpack through the door. Sidles into the blackness.

He touches the boat. The smooth, rounded wood of the hull. Feels the raised letters of her name, *Mills' Muse*. Feels his grandfather's hand on his shoulder. "Slow and steady," Grandpa says. "That's my boy." Cooper sees his grandfather's arms reaching across the water. Hears the snap of the rod. The spin of the reel. Hears his grandfather collapse to the bottom of the boat. Cooper didn't mean to stand up in the boat. He was trying to help Grandpa. He was only trying to help him.

Cooper kneels by the front wheel of the boat trailer. Digs with both hands in the slit of moonlight. Digs and digs. He digs until his fingertips scrape something hard and cold. With all his might, he pulls the rock from the ground. A rock older than Mr. Bell. The rock his grandfather gave him. The one with the trilobite fossil. The oldest rock in the universe. The grandfather rock.

Cooper buried the rock after Grandpa died. After they took Grandpa away. When there was nothing you could do about it.

He holds the rock like a baby. Hugs it and rocks.

Rocks the rock. "I didn't mean to," Cooper says. "I'm sorry." From now on he will keep the ancient rock next to the other big rock and the two small rocks and the little one, the size of a nickel. The rock family will be as whole as it can be.

Cooper sets the rock on the seat in the stern. He climbs into the boat. Lays his pillow next to the rock. Covers himself with the fishing blanket. Hears the loon calling and calling. Waits for a falling star. This dark place is better than Grandpa's room. It is Grandpa's favorite place in the world.

He opens a juice box. Takes a sip.

Sip, sip, sip.

Lap, lap, lap.

Sleep.

A giant bug sputters in Cooper's ear. He opens his eyes. Squints at the bright sliver of sunlight. He does not know where he is until he breathes. Sniffs. No, there is no giant bug in his ear. The buzz is a jet ski. Cooper remembers where he is. And he is hungry. He thinks of Mr. Bell. *Logic, preparation, and caution.* Glad he prepared, he pulls graham crackers and juice from his backpack. He could live in this boathouse cave happily. Forever. Except he would like to use the outhouse.

The bite of graham cracker crunches in his ear. Crunches like footsteps. *Crunch, crunch, crunch.* Just like footsteps. Exactly like footsteps. He takes another bite. Does not know he hears true footsteps until a kick hits the boathouse door and the door pushes against the sand. Light fills the boathouse except for a tall, black silhouette. He has a visitor. Could it be Mike?

"Mike?" Cooper says.

"We've been looking all over for you," the happy voice says.

No. The visitor is not Mike.

The visitor is The Father.

And his happy voice is fake. Like the caddis fly.

Cooper doesn't answer. His mouth is full of graham cracker.

"You scared your mother. She didn't know where you were. She even called the police." The Father puts his hands on the bow of *Mills' Muse*. "I told her not to worry. I told her I'd find you. And here you are."

Cooper didn't mean to scare his mother. Did not mean to scare anyone. Did not mean to do anything wrong. He can blame That Boy. That Boy complicates things. That Boy wants to stomp his leg. Wants to wash. Cooper holds his knees together. Sits on his hands. Feels the graham cracker break into a million pieces beneath him.

The Father slides his hands along the boat's gunwales to the stern. His shadow slides across Cooper's legs. He pats the antique motor behind Cooper's head. "You miss her, don't you?"

Her, Cooper thinks. *Mills' Muse.* No. He does not have to miss her. The boat is right here. The boat is not an illusion. Cooper misses *him.* He misses his grandfather.

"Me too. Whaddya say we take her out? Do a little fishing. We're lucky it's such a beautiful day."

Cooper does not feel lucky. He feels like Jack's fish. Baited and trapped in the net.

"I can help you with all this, Cooper. Whatever's going on. You just have to let me." The Father sighs. "Talk to me."

Cooper cannot talk to The Father. Cannot tell anyone his secret. No one will ever understand. Especially The Father.

With all his might, The Father pushes both boathouse doors wide open. They squeak and scrape against the sand. "C'mon, Coop. Help me pull this ol' girl into the water. I'll use one of Grandpa's rods.

You're big enough to use mine. We can get breakfast across the lake. Have a nice little chat."

The Father pulls on the boat. The trailer's wheels screech. Screech in pain. Screech like they're holding onto the boat for dear life. The Father huffs and groans.

Cooper sees his fishing rod floating away. Grandpa reaching and reaching. Grandpa's shirt on fire. He remembers swimming. Hard and cold. Pulling on his grandfather's arm. Coming up for air. Hollering at the shore. Swimming with all his might.

Now The Father pushes the boat. Cooper grabs onto the gunwales. Feels his body jerk forward. Jerked into the bright light. He reaches for the big rock. Squints in the sun. The rock is heavy in his hands. He cannot cover his eyes. Cannot cover his ears. He cannot help pull this ol' girl into the water. He will not go back into the water.

Ever.

The boat moves forward.

Cooper leaps from the stern. Lands in the dead weeds washed ashore. The thick and heavy dead reeds that grab at his ankles. He crawls to the safe, dry sand.

"C'mon," The Father says again. He kicks off his shoes. Rolls up his pants. Pushes the boat off the trailer. The bow bobs in the lake. Glides forward. Deeper and deeper. Slides like melting ice cream. Without a sound. "I've got it now. Get back in."

Cooper does not get back in. He doesn't move.

"Cooper."

Cooper doesn't answer.

"Get in," The Father says again. "Get in now." Mad is growing in his voice. "C'mon, I can't hold it steady forever."

But Cooper can hold onto the grandfather rock forever. Forever and ever. And this time he will.

The Father drops the anchor into the water. It splashes like a bomb. The white, lacy water rises in slow motion. "You're getting in this boat if it kills me!" The Father says.

That word. *Kills.* Cooper imagines the grandfather. Dead. Nothing you can do about it. *Don't think about that word. Don't think about that word. Don't think about that word.*

Too late.

Here comes That Boy again. He wants to wash. Wants to count—the waves, the dead reeds, the gnats, every grain of sand. Cooper is glad his arms are full. Please, not now. *Go away*, he thinks to That Boy. *Go away. Go away.* "Go away," he says out loud.

"You don't talk to your father like that, Cooper!"

Cooper feels The Father's arms close around him like ropes. Like the coiled black cord of the phone. Twisted tight until he cannot breathe. He kicks his legs—like a frog. Kicks and kicks. The grandfather rock is yanked from his arms. Thrown. It lands in the water. Sinks to the bottom of the lake.

Drops of water splash Cooper's foot. They burn cold like fire. Cooper feels the burn rise into his throat. Into his nose. He gags. He gets away. Crawling. Crawling until he feels The Father's hands clasp his ankles.

A voice. A sad and crying voice. A voice from the hill.

"Dad! Dad, stop!"

But The Father does not stop.

Does not stop. Does not stop. Does not stop.

"I'm bigger than you are, Cooper." He shoves his hands under Cooper's stomach. Grabs him like a giant claw. Carries Cooper toward the boat. Into the water.

"Dad!" Caddie's voice from the hill. "Just let him go."

"Go inside, Caddie. I can handle this myself."

"But why?" she cries. Caddie runs down the hill.

"Because," The Father breathes hard. "Because if I say he's getting in the boat,"—he fights with Cooper's kicking legs, fights and fights and fights— "he's getting in the boat."

"Mom!" The shout is loud. As loud as a tornado warning.

His mother. She is coming. She will be here any second.

A burn creeps through Cooper. He chokes and gags and spits. Feels another burn. A different burn. A burn that seeps across his lap. Its warmth runs down his leg and across his foot. Drips in the sand.

"David!" his mother screeches.

"What?" The Father says. "What?"

This time when Cooper wriggles free, he falls to the ground.

Caddie stands there. His mother stands there. They have horror in their faces like beautiful movie stars in a thriller. No one knows what they see until it is too late.

Except for Cooper.

And The Father.

"Go home," Caddie says, like a mean friend. Like

she does not want to play with The Father anymore. "Just leave him alone and go home."

"I'm sorry," The Father says. "I didn't mean . . . Cooper—"

"Don't, David," his mother says. "Not now."

Cooper looks up. Sees the burn seep across The Father's face. Sees it sting his eyes. Sees the sadness and the anger. And the fear. Sees him not know what to do. Sees him feel exactly how Cooper feels.

The Father whispers to his mother.

His mother shakes her head.

Cooper crawls to the reeds. To the edge of the water. The grandfather rock lies lifeless at the bottom of the lake. Dead. There is nothing you can do about it now. Cooper pounds the sand with his fist. *Pound. Pound. Pound.*

Caddie kneels in the wet sand. Puts her hand on Cooper's back. Her hand is warmer than the sunlight. "What is it, Coop?"

He points.

"What? All I see is a big rock."

Cooper nods. Shivers. Puts his head down on the dried reeds. Closes his eyes.

"Sure, Cooper. Sure." Caddie wades into the water. Picks up the drowned rock.

The screen door creaks open and snaps shut. In the distance the old boat trailer's wheels screech. Screech and screech. Then the fancy black car rumbles away. The pump brays. There is no day between morning and night. Only sadness. And more whispers. His mother fills the old tub with warm water. Knocks on the door when he is done. Brings him a peanut butter and jelly sandwich. Tucks him into bed.

When she is gone, Cooper lines up his rocks on the black stripe of Grandpa's red blanket—the big, cold damp rock with the trilobite fossil; the smooth one the size of his fist, the size of his heart; the two small ones, like cardinal eggs; and the little one, flat like a nickel—and reads.

With his flashlight, he huddles under the covers. He reads every word, every line, every page, and every chapter. Three times. He reads so The Father will not burn up from the inside out. So his mother and Caddie will not turn to ash. So the world will not blow up and burn like an inferno, killing everyone and destroying everything in its path.

A knock.

"Cooper?"

"What?" He tugs the covers away from his face.

Caddie opens his door. Leans in. Looks at Amicus, eye-to-eye. "I'd forgotten all about him."

"That is easy to do with small things," Cooper says.

She taps on the glass of the aquarium. "I just wanted to say good night."

"To Amicus the Great?"

"No, Cooper. To you."

Today Caddie has been his knight. She has rescued him. As soon as she leaves, he will write this in his notebook:

It does not feel good to be rescued. Being rescued feels like holding all the world's worry in one pocket.

"I'm sorry," he says.

Caddie shakes her head. "You don't have to be sorry. It's not your fault. You didn't do anything wrong."

"What about the policeman?"

Caddie tilts her head in the air. Looks at the ceiling. "I was talking about Dad. And I'm sorry. I'm sorry it all happened."

"You're my hero," he says. "Someday I will make it up to you."

"Whatever you do, please don't," she says.

Cooper doesn't answer. Someday he will make it up to her. Truer than true.

Even Amicus the Great is silent.

"It's a joke, Coop." She smiles, but Cooper can't smile back. "Really, Cooper, don't worry about it. You can't help it. Some things just are the way they are and there's nothing you can do about it. You have to believe me."

"I believe you," he says. Because everything Caddie says really is getting more and more believable every day.

He picks up his pencil and opens his notebook, thinking. But what if there *is* something he can do about it? What if there *was* something? What if there *could be* something? How will he ever know for sure?

"Good night, Coop."

"Good night, Caddie."

Caddie closes the door.

Cooper writes,

You must never give up unless you know for sure.

NEWS

Cooper wakes up to the gulping sound of a frog croaking. "Good morning Amicus the Great," he whispers, getting out of bed. He drops one food nugget into the aquarium. It lands on the plastic lily pad, bounces into the water. Cooper waits for Amicus to snap it up, yawns, and leaves his room.

"Listen to this," Caddie says, flattening *The North Lakes News* across the dining room table. "The suspect, an unidentified minor, is believed to be responsible for a series of local break-ins and may be part of a larger burglary ring that has worked the popular resort area for more than six months. The suspect's family is cooperating fully with the law."

Caddie takes a bite of crunchy cereal. She reads with her mouth full and one finger on the words. "The suspect is being held in the Lake County Jail."

She swallows. "The Loch Ness Monster is locked up where he belongs. And I hope Mike is in there with him." Caddie folds up the newspaper. "Geez. That was a whole week ago. Nothing like up-to-the-minute news." She waves the newspaper in the air. "Cooper, you should read this. You were right all along."

Cooper does not want to read the newspaper. Does not want to read about The Grinner. Does not care that he was right. The Grinner is not a happy thought. *Poor Mike. Poor Mike. Poor Mike.* Mike is not a happy thought either.

Think a happy thought.

Ice cream is a happy thought.

Ice cream. Ice cream. Ice cream.

His mother comes out of the kitchen with a pink towel wrapped around her head. She looks like a giant cone of cotton candy. "Can we go into town and get ice cream?" Cooper asks.

"Now?" their mother says.

Caddie drinks the milk from her bowl. Swallows. Wipes a drip from her chin. "Yeah. I want to get some new earrings before we go home."

"I guess I could get a few groceries," their mother says. She unwinds the towel, shakes her dark hair loose and free. "Just to get us through the last few days up here. Hard to believe we're going home so soon." Her big pink comb with giant teeth cuts through her tangled hair. Makes it smooth. "Would you like to get a souvenir, Cooper? Maybe some moccasins? Or do something you've always wanted to?" She squeezes the wet ends of her hair in the towel. "Maybe we could all play miniature golf," she says.

"No, thank you," Caddie says. She makes a funny face at Cooper. A face their mother cannot see.

Cooper blinks his eyes at Caddie. He does not want to return to the scene of the crime. "Just ice cream," he says. Caddie smiles.

"I mean something we haven't done yet. Anything you want."

"I will think about it," Cooper says. And he does. Maybe he will buy something he has not always wanted. He will buy something at Ron's Bait Shop. He will buy the vest with a hundred pockets. A souvenir of his old friend Mike.

When it's time to go into town, Cooper lifts up Amicus's aquarium. Pulls out the five flat twenties Mike paid him for tying flies. He taps them three times and folds them into his pocket.

Caddie grabs the car keys on the hook by the back door. "I'm driving," she says. "You hardly let me drive all summer."

The screen door squeaks open. Snaps shut.

Caddie puts on her seat belt. Starts the engine.

Cooper puts on his seat belt. So does his mother. "Adjust your mirrors, Caddie," she says. The van lurches forward. Cooper grabs the door handle. Wonders if he is hanging on for dear life. *Don't think about driving. Don't think about driving. Don't think about driving.*

"Don't go so fast," their mother says.

"Mom," Caddie says.

Now the trees go by so slowly, Cooper could count them. He closes his eyes. *Don't count. Don't count. Don't count.*

"Turn here," their mother says when they pass the gas station.

"Mom," Caddie says again. And then the car bumps against the curb in front of Grandma's Goods Antiques & Collectibles. Caddie pulls the keys from the ignition. Puts them in her purse. "I'm driving home too," she says.

"Keep the change," his mother says when she hands Cooper a five-dollar bill. She looks at her watch. "It's twenty to four. Meet me back here in one hour."

"Okay," Cooper says. "Four forty on the dot."

His mother goes into the antique store. Caddie has already crossed the street.

Today "tourist trap" is an oxymoron. The parking spaces are empty. The sidewalks are not bustling. Cooper is the only one in line at The Whole Scoop ice cream stand. They are out of chocolate. And cookie dough. He orders a sugar cone with two scoops of mint ice cream and three napkins because it is a very hot day. He watches the door of Ron's Bait Shop across the road. "I'm in a hurry," he says to the clerk.

He runs to the corner with his ice cream cone. Licks the green ice cream. Waits for the pickup truck with the trailer. Waits for the motorhome. Licks his ice cream cone. Waits for the SUV towing the yellow speedboat. Thinks of tourists as birds. Migrating. The flocks are all flying in one direction. South. Everyone is going home. Summer is almost over. He licks the ice cream cone again. Catches the pale green drip running down his thumb.

Out of breath, Cooper arrives in the parking lot of Ron's Bait Shop. He reads the sign on the door.

PLEASE NO FOOD OR DRINK

He turns around. Licks his ice cream cone in a circle. Catches every drip. Looks at fishing lures and bobbers and hats on a table outside the door.

END OF SUMMER SALE 50% OFF

At the edge of the parking lot, he spots an enormous contraption he has never seen before. Not even on Tezorene. It is other-worldly. Perhaps a spaceship. Cooper circles the mysterious structure. Eight big metal cans, like garbage cans, are covered with wooden planks. He kicks one rusty orange can. It bellows like a whale. Full of air. The contraption appears to be some kind of floating device.

It is a raft.

Cooper licks his ice cream cone.

The raft has a white tag taped to one of the orange tanks.

The raft is for sale.

Cooper circles the raft again. He thinks of Tom Sawyer and his gang of pirates. Thinks of the Jolly Roger. Thinks of Caddie, who would like to float on something. Of Mr. Bell, who would like to do it all over again if he had the chance. Cooper has an idea. His knees shake with excitement. He will not buy the vest with a hundred pockets. He will buy the raft. He turns over the price tag.

FOR SALE
~~$400.00~~ ~~$350.00~~ ~~$200.00~~ $150.00

No, he will not buy the raft. He can't afford the raft. He will buy what he came for. He will buy Jack's vest. Cooper looks to the window high up in Ron's Bait Shop.

The vest is gone. *Gone, gone, gone.* Like Grandpa. Like summer. Like his friend Mike. Everything is gone. Cooper turns in circles. He looks at the window. Looks at the sun. Looks at the front door of Ron's Bait Shop. He wants to run. Wants to wash. With his free hand, he counts the rivets on the orange raft. *One, two, three, four, five, six, seven . . .*

No counting. No counting. No counting.

. . . eight, nine, ten . . .

Think a happy thought. Think a happy thought. Think a happy—

The bell tinkles. Someone is coming through the door of Ron's Bait Shop. Someone carrying two big blue bags of garbage. It can't be Mike, but it *is* Mike. Mike is carrying garbage to the dumpster.

Cooper's knees shake all over again. "Mike!" he yells.

Mike slows. Turns. Turns back.

"Over here!" Cooper eats the pointy tip of his ice cream cone.

Mike turns around again. Finally sees Cooper in the bright sun. "Oh," Mike says. "Hi." Like they are strangers. Like he's never seen Cooper before in his whole life.

Cooper's heart sinks. Mike is not the same. Mike has changed.

Mike swings one garbage bag to the right, and then to the left, higher, then to the right, and finally up and over his head and into the dumpster.

"You're not in jail!" Cooper yells. He follows the edge of the parking lot to the dumpster. "I told the policeman you weren't the bad guy."

Mike doesn't answer. He picks up the second bag of garbage. Swings it into the dumpster. Something is wrong with Mike. Very wrong.

Cooper wipes his hands. Wads up the napkins. Throws them into the dumpster. "It's my fault," Cooper says.

Mike walks away.

Cooper follows. "Mike," he says, louder this time. "It's my fault."

Mike straightens the fishing hats and lures on the table. "Cooper," he says, "where's your mom?"

"Grocery shopping."

"Why don't you go help her. I'm busy."

"I just wanted to say I'm sorry."

"You don't have to be sorry, Cooper. Just leave me alone."

Cooper's insides shudder with sadness. Mike is the most confusing Earthling Cooper has ever met. He wants to stomp his leg. He wants to wash. He does not want to do any of these things or he might scare Mike away. "But I'm your friend," Cooper says. "Friends look out for each other."

Mike's shoulders slump. He shakes his head. "I am not your friend, Cooper."

"Yes, you are."

Mike shakes his head again. This time he shakes it the way Caddie does when she wants Cooper to go away. "I'm too old to be your friend."

"No one is too old to be a friend. I have a friend named Mr. Bell. I believe he is many decades older than you are."

Mike shrugs. "Everyone is friends with Mr. Bell."

"Then my hypothesis is true."

"That's not what I mean, Cooper." Mike sighs.

"Then you can be my unlikely friend."

Mike turns away. Opens the door. The bell tinkles overhead. "Cooper, I can't talk to you right now." Mike points at a sign taped to the glass.

NO LOITERING

Mike is being mean. The national anthem of Tezorene plays in Cooper's head. *O Tezorene, where no one's mean* . . . Mike should visit Tezorene. "I should have warned you," Cooper says.

Mike stops. Shakes his head again. He turns around with exasperation in his hands, in his face, all over his body. "About what?"

"About The Grinner." Mike makes a funny face. "Your friend," Cooper says.

Mike is still confused.

"About Todd," Cooper says.

Now Mike makes a face like something smells bad. "Friend, right." Mike goes into the back room of the bait shop. "How would you have known?"

Cooper follows. "I just knew, so it's all my fault."

"That doesn't make a lick of sense," Mike says. He pulls a big blue plastic garbage bag from a box. Snaps it open in the air. "If anyone should have known, I should have known. We'd been best friends since kindergarten." Mike fills the bag with wrappers and boxes and broken things. "He was stealing from people we know. People who were friends. He even stole from me and my dad."

My dad and me, Cooper thinks as fast as he can, but he doesn't say anything.

"I just couldn't see it." Mike ties off another big blue bag of garbage. Hoists it to his shoulder.

Cooper wishes he had a best friend since kindergarten. A friend no matter what. A friend like Mike. "It is a very unfortunate situation," Cooper says.

"I don't know what happened. Maybe I could have helped him."

"It's not your fault," Cooper says. "Some things are just the way they are and there's nothing you can do about it."

Mike snorts through his nose. A disappointed kind of snort. "My dad always says things get worse before they get better. But it's hard. It's like liking a girl who doesn't like you back." Cooper follows Mike through the bait shop. He holds the door open for Mike and his bag of garbage. The bell tinkles over their heads. "You can't see it but everyone else can. It feels terrible when you finally figure it out." Mike looks down at Cooper. "Be glad you don't know about these things yet."

"You mean a girl like Caddie?"

"No. I mean yes. I mean . . . No. She's nice." Mike walks faster and faster toward the dumpster. "Let's not talk about her. You should go."

"People are illusions," Cooper says.

Mike sets down the bag of garbage. "What's that supposed to mean?" He picks up a big cardboard box next to the dumpster. Pulls open the flaps, rips its seams, and flattens the box under his arms.

"Illusions are erroneous perceptions of reality," Cooper says. "They aren't what you think they are."

Mike nods his head and sails the cardboard box into the dumpster. Swallows. Makes his lips look angry. "You're a pretty smart kid."

"Some people believe I am a mutant."

Mike snorts again. This time it is a happy, laughing kind of snort. He picks up the blue bag of garbage. "Nah, Cooper," he says, swinging the bag to his left, "you're just over here"—he swings the bag to his right—"when most people are over here. It's not like you're from a different planet or anything." He swings the bag in a full circle and heaves it into the dumpster.

"Meep," Cooper says.

Mike laughs. "On second thought, maybe you are."

"I made you laugh," Cooper says. "Does that mean we are friends again?" Cooper runs and climbs up on the raft. "Ahoy," he calls to Mike. "Bring her to the wind!" he shouts into a pretend gale.

Mike shakes his head. Throws his hands in the air. "What sails does she have?" Mike shouts back.

"No, Mike. You're supposed to say, 'What sails she carrying?'"

Mike walks closer to the raft. "Sorry. I haven't read *Tom Sawyer* in a long time."

"Get up here, Mike." Cooper cups his hand to his brow. Points to the moccasin shop across the street. "Land ho!"

Mike laughs again and pulls himself up on the raft. "'What sails she carrying?'"

Cooper looks to the sky. "'Course, tops'ls and flying jib, sir.'"

"Aye-aye," Mike says. "I take it you're done with the book."

"No, I ain't," Cooper says. "I reckon I'm a slow reader."

"So if you thought I was in jail, what are you doing here?" Mike jumps to the pavement.

"I came to make a purchase."

"To buy this proud seafaring ship?" Mike kicks one of the tanks. It bellows like a whale.

"No, sir," Cooper says. "She's a fine vessel indeed, but I can't afford her. Besides, she doesn't have a mast." He puts his hands on his hips. "And I am not a seagoing lad. I am here to buy a vest like Jack's." Cooper points to the empty window. "But it's gone."

"Then bring her round to port," Mike says. "And come with me."

Cooper jumps down from the raft. The bell tinkles over their heads as they enter the bait shop. "We sold that one, but I think we have one left. And it's on sale."

Cooper follows Mike up to the counter. The shelves look like the shelves in the empty refrigerator at the cabin. "Your store is going hungry," Cooper says.

"It always looks like this at the end of the season," Mike says.

The bell tinkles again. A customer wants a fishing hat. "Just a minute, Cooper." Mike rings up the sale. The cash register chirps and slams. And then Mike climbs a ladder. Opens a cupboard and takes out a fluffy plastic bag. "Shoot, it's an extra-large. But it's the last one."

"That's okay," Cooper says. "I'm growing like a weed. How much do I owe you?"

"Forty-seven fifty-six," Mike says. He rings up the sale. The cash register chirps and slams.

Cooper hands him three of his five twenties. "Keep the change."

Mike shakes his head. "Can't do that, Cooper. It wouldn't be right."

"But that way you could take Caddie on a date."

"Like she'd go out with me."

"I think she likes you," Cooper says.

Mike shakes his head again. His cheeks turn as red as a fishing bobber. He hands Cooper a ten-dollar bill, two ones, and change. Cooper puts the coins in the little black dish by the cash register. He turns Alexander Hamilton's face right side up. George Washington's too. Matches the corners of the ten-dollar bill and the ones to the corners of his two twenties. He feels Mike's eyes on his hands. Feels

Mike pretend he isn't watching. "You are a good friend, Mike," Cooper says.

Mike smiles. "With a vest like that, you'll have to let me take you fishing."

Cooper shakes his head. "We're going home in five days."

"Oh," Mike says. "Maybe next year."

Cooper knows he will never go fishing. Never go in the water. Never, ever again. "Maybe you can take Caddie," Cooper says.

"Cooper," Mike says, just the way Caddie says his name. With a very long "ooo."

"What? She's a nice girl."

"I know she is," Mike says. "Can you say good-bye to her for me?"

"I reckon I'd be happy to." But suddenly Cooper has another idea. His knees begin to shake like a malt maker. *Mind your own business. Mind your own business. Mind your own business.* "Just a minute," he says. "I don't want to forget something." Cooper takes out his notebook and his pencil and writes this down:

It's hard to mind your own business when you know you can make a difference.

He reads the sentence over again. Knows he is being sneaky. Knows he must convince Mike his idea is the truth. "Now I remember," Cooper says. "It says right here. I'm supposed to invite you to our party."

"Really?" Mike says. "You're really having a party?" Mike tries to read Cooper's sentence. Cooper closes the notebook just in time.

A party is a good idea. A very good idea. A party is something Cooper hasn't done all summer. That's what he will tell his mother he wants to do. It is the happiest thought he can think of.

Cooper nods. "We're having a going-away party."

"For yourselves?" Mike says.

Cooper nods. "An ice cream party. You can be my guest."

"When is it?"

Cooper opens his notebook again. Pretends to find the date among his words. "The day after tomorrow. At seven o'clock sharp. Can you come?"

Mike looks at the leaping fish clock on the wall.

Cooper looks at the leaping fish clock. The time is four forty-seven. He is late. He hurries for the door.

"I think I can," Mike says.

"Then I reckon I better finish *The Adventures of Tom Sawyer.*" The bell tinkles. "Goodbye, Mike," he says. He hugs his package. Runs across the road. Spots Caddie in her new dangly earrings. Meets his mother coming out of the grocery store.

"What have you got there?" she asks.

Cooper waits to answer. Waits until they catch up to Caddie at the van. "I have an idea. I know one last thing to do before we go home. Something we haven't done all summer."

"What?" Caddie asks.

"It's a surprise."

"Yeah, but what's the surprise?"

"I'm not telling." Cooper gets in the back seat. Feels the smile on his face like a hundred leaping fish.

His mother turns around. "Cooper, sometimes you have to tell what the surprise is so people can be prepared."

"Then it won't be a surprise," he says.

Caddie stops at the stop sign at the end of town. Looks at him in the rearview mirror. "But your surprises are different from other people's surprises," she says.

Another idea pops up like a tickle in Cooper's brain. "Then I have some news."

"It better be good news," Caddie says.

"I'm having an ice cream party. The day after tomorrow at seven o'clock in the evening. We will need to buy supplies."

His mother looks at Caddie. Caddie rolls her eyes. "Oh, boy," Caddie says. "A party with the three of us. That'll be exciting."

Now Cooper has another idea. "Mr. Bell will be my guest of honor." He has a secret too. A secret he cannot tell about a secret guest named Mike. A secret surprise for Caddie.

"Mr. Bell is a very sick man," his mother says.

"I have to try," Cooper says.

He watches out the window. Watches for the yard with the big black bell. "Turn here," he says.

Caddie and his mother wait for him in the idling car, parked by the old garage. The gravel crunches beneath Cooper's feet the rest of the way to Mr. Bell's house. He puts his finger in the loops of the fancy B on Mr. Bell's door. Pushes the doorbell one, two, three times. Mary Ann opens the door with a frown on her face.

"Is Mr. Bell home?"

Mary Ann looks over her shoulder. Whispers, "He's sleeping right now."

Cooper whispers too. "Please tell Mr. Bell he is cordially invited to my ice cream party the day after tomorrow at seven o'clock sharp. Tell him he may bring you as his special guest."

"I'm afraid Mr. Bell isn't feeling very well. I'm afraid . . ."

Afraid.

Cooper is afraid too.

Cooper is afraid Mary Ann will say no. Afraid Mr. Bell will be too sick to come. He feels That Boy standing next to him. He wants to stomp his leg. But he must outsmart That Boy. He puts his finger in the loops of the fancy B one at a time. He talks fast. Faster than his fingers can move. "Mr. Bell isn't afraid of anything. And ice cream is his favorite food. Please tell Mr. Bell I look forward to seeing him." Mary Ann nods, but the frown is still on her face. "Watch for the red mailbox. The one that says 'Mills.'"

Cooper gasps for air.

Mary Ann does not smile. "I'll do my best," she says.

Cooper does not smile. He is too busy thinking.

Thinking about that word, *afraid*. He walks toward the car thinking. He steps on the path of pine needles and sand, one foot at a time. Thinking. He steps on a dry oak leaf. And another. Thinking. Thinking about pepperoni pizza. Thinking about The Grinner. Thinking about the dead ivy and the sharp tip of its green wire. Thinking about The Father. And fishing.

He thinks about tying flies.

Pictures the grandfather, reaching and reaching.

His memories are as clear as the big window in Mr. Bell's house.

His memories are like the pictures on Mr. Bell's wall.

Don't think. Don't think. Don't think.

He stops walking. Looks to the sky. But he cannot stop thinking.

He thinks of the eagle soaring across the lake. There is no picture of the eagle on Mr. Bell's wall. Not yet. He walks backward. Thinking about all the things that have happened behind him. He turns as if he can see everything in Mr. Bell's memory window. Turns again, thinking. Walks forward.

He thinks about that word, *forward*.

Thinks about all the things that haven't happened yet.

There is tonight. There is tomorrow. There is the day after tomorrow at seven o'clock sharp.

He feels the tremble start in his toes and follow his nerve endings all the way up to his brain. Backward. And forward. It takes only a second.

He cannot remember the last time he looked forward.

CHANGE

"Look at that tree," Cooper's mother says. "It's already turning." She spreads her beach towel on the sand next to Caddie's. "I can't believe it. The leaves are already changing color."

Cooper studies the birch tree. Its yellow leaves flutter like the flames of a burning candle. "It's because of the drought," he says. "It hasn't rained in weeks. I should have watered it."

"Cooper," Caddie says. "Birch trees are dying out all over Minnesota. There's nothing you can do about it. Besides, you're not in charge of the trees. You . . ." She points a knitting needle at the new enormous sandcastle. His magnum opus. "You have enough to do as the leader of Tezorene."

Today the sands of Tezorene rise to Cooper's waist. Taller than Caddie as she sits knitting in the sun. Knitting the world's longest scarf with their mother's leftover yarn. He stands on the dry reeds. Fills the red bucket with cool water at the edge of the lake. "I am not the leader of Tezorene. I am the mastermind. There is a difference."

His mother wraps her arms around her knees and stares across the calm lake. "I can't believe we'll be closing up the cabin in just a few days. School will start and the next thing you know, it'll be winter."

"Don't remind me," Caddie says.

"Don't remind me," Cooper says. He has not thought about school. Has not thought about teachers and classmates. About the stares and whispers. He does not look forward to school. *Don't think about school. Don't think about school. Don't think about school. Think a happy thought. Hurry. Think a happy thought before That Boy has a chance to show up and ruin everything. Tezorene is a happy thought.* Cooper hums the national anthem of Tezorene, *O, Tezorene, where no one's mean,* as loud as he can. Over and over again.

"Cooper," Caddie says, "you're driving me crazy with that stupid song."

Cooper fills his red bucket with water.

Earthlings have traveled far and united with the

Tezornauts. They have brought with them many tanks of Aitch-Two-Oh and many vats of chocolate because Tezorene is hot and nothing tastes better than melted chocolate. Soldiers can live for a long time on chocolate and Aitch-Two-Oh. Cooper has read this in a book.

The Earthlings and the Tezornauts will fight ozone-eating larvae of the oxydiptera. Tezorene has an infestation of the dreadful insect. A gift of trickery from a devious and hostile planet. Together the warriors will spray the air with boiling water until every last fluttering wing is downed.

It is okay because it is pretend.

Gnats cloud Cooper's face. He waves them away. Spits in the sand. Gets another bucket of precious water for Tezorene.

"How about hot dogs for lunch?" their mother says. She lies on her beach towel, on her back. Her crossed arms cover her face.

"Meep-meep," Cooper says with Tezornaut joy.

"Cooper," Caddie says. "Not this again."

His mother rolls onto her stomach. "And then I think we better go shopping for your party, Cooper. Get that ice cream underway. What kind do you want to make?"

"Chocolate," he says because he knows the Tezornauts might use up all the imported cocoa beans and there won't be any chocolate left for the humans if they do not hurry.

"I invited Dad," their mother says. "I thought he might like to be here for the last few days." She scoops a handful of sand as if it is gold dust and lets it sift through the air. "He was happy to hear the party was your idea, Coop."

"Meep," Cooper says in a really low tone.

"Cooper," Caddie says. "I'm warning you."

He has been warned. He must defend himself. He must pour the bucket of water on Caddie. He knows she will scream and run and chase him. He needs to prove himself as a heroic warrior to the Tezornauts. He can't help it. He dribbles the water on her toes.

"Cooper!" she says. But she does not look up. She is busy knitting her magnum opus. He pours every last drop of the aitch-two-oh on her legs. "Cooper," she says, knitting furiously.

"Caddie," he says, "look!"

This time Caddie does look up. Looks up to see Cooper holding the bucket, the empty bucket— holding it as if it is heavy and full of water. "Hee-yah!"

he says and heaves a bucketful of pretend water at her face. A single drop lands on her ankle, but she cowers and screams. "Cooper!"

He laughs and runs.

His mother laughs too. Cooper stops running and watches her. She has not laughed in a very long time. He says, "Hee-yah," again and she laughs more and more.

A phone rings beyond the hill. They all turn their heads, listening. "That's our phone," Caddie says.

"I suppose I should get it," their mother says. She stands. Steps into her flip-flops. Walks slowly up the hill. The phone rings again.

"I bet that's Dad," Caddie says in her whisper voice. "You wanna bet he can't make it?"

"Why would we wager on something we know to be true?"

"It's just a saying, Cooper. Don't be so literal."

He picks up a dead sand spider with a stick. "Look," he says.

"Don't you dare," Caddie says.

The flying arachnid lands atop Tezorene. Leaps from its ship. The oxydiptera have mutated. Grown exponentially. This emergency calls for more aitch-two-oh. Cooper fills the bucket. Accidentally spills the water near Caddie's foot.

"Cooper! I said, don't."

"It was an accident. I am attempting to eradicate the oxydiptera."

"There is no such thing as oxydiptera."

"You mean *are*. And you are wrong. Oxydiptera are alive and well on Tezorene. Unfortunately."

Their mother is gone a long time. Caddie's scarf is longer than ever. And the oxydiptera have been eradicated. Tezorene is free. Aitch-two-oh has brought new and unexpected life to Tezorene.

"The hot dogs are ready," their mother calls from the top of the hill.

"Can we have a picnic on the beach?" Cooper calls back.

"Not today," she says. "Please come up here."

Cooper hears sadness in his mother's voice. More sadness than ever. Cooper knows Caddie is right: The Father is not coming. Cooper is right too: a bet was unnecessary. Cooper thinks of the big rock at home on his desk. He imagines it alone. Forever.

Tezorene sizzles. The sand dries up like dust. The mastermind stands frozen on the blistering hot grounds of Tezorene. The Father must still be angry.

He doesn't know how hard Cooper has worked to be good. *So hard. So hard. So hard.*

But something feels different. Something has changed.

"C'mon, I'm starving," Caddie says.

The hot dogs lie still in their buns like hibernating Tezornauts. They are unaware of impending disaster. The world of Tezorene could come to an end and the hibernating Tezornauts would never know what happened.

Their mother pours the last of the potato chips into a bowl. They crunch like warm lettuce. The ketchup is almost gone.

"Who called?" Caddie asks. She washes her hands at the pump in the kitchen.

"Dad," their mother says, her voice flat.

"You were right," Cooper says to Caddie.

"Let me guess," Caddie says. "He's not coming."

Cooper holds his breath. The potato chip melts on his tongue. Turns to goo. He thinks of Tezorene. Thinks of all the garbage and waste pushed to its center. Smoldering. He pictures himself as the incinerator. Swallows the melted potato chip.

"Oh, Caddie," their mother says. Her eyes glisten. Cooper hears a secret in the single breath between her words. She wipes the sticky ketchup bottle with a paper towel. "Here," she says. "I added a little water to stretch it."

Caddie carries the ketchup bottle to the dining room table. "Well, is he?" She leans over her chair. Picks up a hot dog. Squirts it with runny ketchup.

Their mother shakes her head. Looks at the paper towel smeared with ketchup. "No, he's not," she says, "but . . ."

Cooper sits down. He knows the paper towel has blurred to nothingness in his mother's eyes. He takes a bite of his hot dog. Watches. Waits. Listens.

"But what?" Caddie says. "What?"

Caddie and his mother move like robots in slow motion. Caddie sits down. Takes a bite of her hot dog. His mother squeezes the paper towel. Turns toward the kitchen. A bird lands on the windowsill, flies away.

"He won't be living at home when we get back."

Cooper saw this secret coming. Again, he thinks of the big rock at home on his desk. Alone. He should have brought it to the cabin. He should have kept the family whole. He should have worked harder to be good. He chews his bite of hot dog one, two, three times on one side. Turns his head so no one will notice. Hopes no one will see That Boy sitting in the chair next to him at the table. He chews his hot dog one, two, three times on the other side.

"What?" Caddie says.

"I asked him to leave," their mother says from the kitchen.

Cooper stops chewing.

"What do you mean?" Caddie leans back in her chair, hard. Her chair creaks. "Are you getting a divorce? Is that what you mean?"

Cooper is afraid. Afraid to listen. He wants to count. He wants to run to his room and read, three times three times three. But he cannot leave Caddie in her hour of need. He needs to be her hero. He must stay strong. He cannot let his fear show.

Caddie's hands shake. Her voice shrinks to a tiny murmur. "Are you?"

Cooper imagines Caddie at the top of a roller coaster. He can't reach her. What if she falls? What if he can't catch her?

Their mother comes to the table. "We don't know yet," she says with serious eyes. "We just know things need to change."

Falling, falling, falling.

"I had hoped," their mother says, "but—"

"It's my fault, isn't it? It's all my fault because I told him to go home." Caddie throws her hot dog on her plate. Folds her arms. Blinks back tears. Looks down.

"It's not your fault," Cooper says. "It's my fault."

"Please. It's nobody's fault," their mother says. She reaches for their hands. "It's been hard for a long time. And when things get harder, it all just gets worse."

Caddie is sad. His mother is sad. The air is silent and heavy with sadness. Cooper thinks of Mike and The Grinner. He pulls a sentence from his memory. "Sometimes things have to get worse before they can get better," he says.

Caddie lifts her head. Squints her wet eyes at him. She takes a deep, shaky breath.

Their mother smiles. A smile so heavy she lets it go. She puts one hand on Cooper's arm, uses the other to wipe tears from her face with the paper towel. A piece of dried ketchup hangs from her eyelash. "That's why sometimes change is for the better." She takes a bite of soft potato chip, spits it into her hand. "These are stale," she says. The bit of dried ketchup falls into the bowl. Lands on a stale potato chip. "I'll get you something else."

Cooper stares at his hot dog until it blurs to

nothingness. *Change, change, change.* Channels change. Gears change. Minds change. Leaves change color and die and then it is winter and then it is spring and leaves come back. People die and do not come back and there is nothing you can do about it.

And some people are erroneous perceptions of reality.

Like That Boy.

Like The Father.

He takes out his pencil.

Sometimes things change when you don't want them to. It is better when change is your own idea.

Their mother brings a plate and two apples to the table. She slices the apples into wedges. Holds a piece to her lips. "We'll just take it step by step," she says. She takes a bite of the apple and goes back to the kitchen. "Do you want some milk?"

Cooper takes another bite of his hot dog. Chews it on the right side one, two, three times. The watery ketchup drips onto his plate. He feels heat in his face. A burn in his eyes. The sting of salt. *Be strong. Be strong. Be strong.* Be strong for Caddie. He puts his hot dog on his plate. Swallows. Looks at Caddie. Tears stream from her red eyes.

"Don't cry, Caddie," he says. He wishes Grandpa were here to make it all better. "Everything will be okay." He pulls another sentence from his memory. "We can't see it right now, but everyone else can."

"See what?" Caddie says.

"That everything's going to be okay. We'll be okay."

"How do you know?"

Cooper doesn't know. He has no idea. No proof. He needs Caddie to tell him they will be okay. If Caddie says it, then it will be true, because everything she says is getting more and more believable every day. But she is falling. Falling from the sky. And he must catch her before she hits the ground. She needs him to catch her.

And he needs her.

He needs her to say everything will be okay.

"Say we'll be okay, Caddie. Just say it." Caddie stares at him. He pounds the table with his fist. One, two, three times. "Please. I need you to say it."

Caddie puts her hand on his fist. Holds it tight. She wipes the tears from her eyes. From her face. "Okay, Cooper. We'll be okay," she says.

Okay, okay, okay. "I knew it," he says. "I knew it. I knew it. We'll be okay."

She smiles.

She believes him.

And he believes her.

Because everything Caddie says is getting more and more believable every day.

We'll be okay, Cooper thinks when they go to the grocery store. *Okay,* he thinks when they buy everything they need to make chocolate ice cream. Strawberry too, because his mother likes strawberry ice cream and Cooper wants her to be happy.

Okay, he thinks when they go back to the beach and Caddie and his mother sit side by side, knitting.

Okay, he thinks when they eat spaghetti for dinner. "Look," their mother says, coming in from the yard, holding one red tomato. "I grew it myself." She cuts it into three pieces. Smiles proudly. "There. A vegetable." Caddie laughs. Then their mother laughs. Then Cooper laughs. But only for a moment. There is still a lot to keep track of.

"Everything will be okay," he says to Amicus when he sits down on his bed and wipes sand from his feet. *Okay,* he thinks if he reads.

He will read to his mother's secrets. To The

Father being alone. To Caddie's sadness. *Okay,* he thinks when he writes this in his notebook:

Sometimes heroes are heroic because they are brave enough to change.

Cooper lays out his rocks at the foot of his bed. The big one with the fossil, the one the size of his fist, the two small ones, and the little flat one. Like a nickel. By tomorrow he must finish *The Adventures of Tom Sawyer* and tell Mike he loved it, just like Mike said he would.

He reads and reads and reads.

Tom Sawyer and Becky Thatcher are still lost in the cave. But maybe Tom has found a way out. Cooper counts the pages—all the way to eighteen. Eighteen times three, times three, equals one hundred and sixty-two. He reads about the funeral and the ransom money. And all about Huck. *Huck, Huck, Huck.* How Huck joins the gang like a respectable fellow.

He reads and reads and reads.

And yawns.

He is almost done with the book. Only one paragraph to go. The paragraph is called "Conclusion." But Cooper is tired. So tired he can't finish. But he must finish. He must finish in time to give the book back to Mike at the ice cream party.

The words on the page turn fuzzy. *So. So. So. Endeth. Endeth. Endeth. This. This. This. Chronicle. Chronicle. Chronicle. So endeth this chronicle.* Cooper stops reading. Counts the lines that remain. Ten. Only ten lines left. He yawns again. He wants to know how the book ends. Wants to know what Samuel Langhorne Clemens has to say to the world. He can't read another word. Must read every word. Three times three. Tonight is his last chance.

He keeps reading.

He reads the next word once. Just once before his eyes begin to close.

His head bobs.

His eyes open.

He looks around the room. At the golden walls. At the dresser. At Amicus the Great.

Everything is the same. Nothing is on fire.

He reads the next word just once.

And waits.

Then the next word, just once.

And waits.

He reads the rest of the sentence. As fast as he can. Just once.

He reads as if he is running. Jumping stone to stone across a rushing river. As if his life depends on it.

All. The. Way. To. The. End.

Done.

Cooper is out of breath. Out of breath and still breathing. Alive.

He dares to look up. Amicus's chest pumps with smokeless breath. Amicus the Great is alive. Cooper gets out of bed. Gets his magnifying glass. Opens his door without a sound. Tiptoes across the hall.

Caddie's elbow glows in the moonlight. She breathes invisible whispers. Cooper inhales deeply. Soundlessly. He does not smell smoke. He holds the magnifying glass above Caddie's head. Does not see sparks of fire in her hair.

But he hears a creak across the cabin. He must check on his mother.

Cooper tiptoes through the living room in the moonlight to the other side of the cabin. He watches his shadow sneak like a robber's across the wall. The robber of life. He has broken his own rules. He has risked the lives of people he loves.

Cooper listens at his mother's door. Hears her sigh in her sleep. When he breathes deeply, all he smells is dish soap. Nothing is burning.

Everyone is still alive.

The cabin is quiet.

The books and the chairs and the lamps and the tables stand still in the moonlight.

Everything is exactly the same.

But everything has changed.

A funny noise.

Cooper tiptoes back to his room. He knew it. Amicus is croaking. Croaking with joy.

A tremble begins in Cooper's toes. Rises in his legs. Sparks in his stomach. He thinks of the glass fishing boat with the dead ivy. The turtle crawling in the wrong direction. The look in the eye of the dying fish. Of Mr. Bell trying to hold his camera steady. His mother's one tomato.

Like a power surge, electricity moves through Cooper's whole body. He imagines himself glowing. Glowing with hope.

SAILING

They're late. They're late. They're late.

Beneath the colossal Norway pines, Cooper watches the driveway for his special guests, rocking foot to foot. He is looking forward. *Forward, forward, forward.*

"Look what I found in a drawer," his mother says.

Cooper looks. His mother is blowing into a yellow balloon.

"What time is it?" Cooper asks.

She pinches the balloon. Looks at her watch. "Seven o-five."

"The party started at seven o'clock sharp," Cooper says.

"That doesn't mean he's late, Cooper," Caddie says, coming outside. "Not yet."

Cooper rocks foot to foot.

"It's okay, Cooper. Mr. Bell might not be up to it," his mother says. She blows into the balloon again. "We can have our own party if he can't come." She ties the yellow balloon to the clothesline. It hangs, like a drop of water, frozen in mid-air.

Cooper does not like looking forward. Looking forward makes him shiver inside. Looking forward feels like being scared.

A white vehicle slows by the mailbox. Could it be Mike? No, it is not a Jeep. It's a van. The van groans. Turns down the driveway. "It's Mr. Bell!" Cooper shouts.

"Who else would it be?" Caddie says.

Mary Ann is driving. Cooper gives Mary Ann a big thumbs-up through the windshield. Waves his hands. Shows Mary Ann where to park under the biggest Norway pine.

Mary Ann gets out of the van. She opens the back end and pulls out a folded-up wheelchair. She opens Mr. Bell's door. The oxygen tank hisses. Mary Ann disconnects the oxygen tank. Carries Mr. Bell as if he is a stiff doll. His plaid fishing hat falls to the ground.

Today Mr. Bell looks like a praying mantis— hunched and thin and pale green. Mr. Bell has changed color with the leaves.

Mary Ann reconnects the oxygen tank. Brushes off his fishing hat and puts it back on his head. Mr. Bell is reassembled.

"Welcome to our abode," Cooper says.

Mary Ann sets Betsy the camera in Mr. Bell's lap. Voices twitter like birds. Mr. Bell is glad to be here. Was here before. Many years ago. Why the last time . . .

Of course, his mother says. She remembers too. And his mother is the spitting image of her mother. What a coincidence. Why is it they never got together sooner? That's just how things go. Hard to believe another summer is almost over.

It seems like yesterday.

Yes, it is hard to believe.

Of course, it is hard to believe.

Time is an illusion.

It's hard to believe Mike will come to the party. If he is coming, he should be here by now. Cooper looks up the driveway. Watches the road through the trees. Watches for the white Jeep with leaping fish painted on its door.

"Cooper? Should we go in and get started?" his mother asks.

"That's a good idea," Mary Ann says. "The sun is hard on Mr. Bell."

"The sun is not hard on Mr. Bell," Mr. Bell says in his crackle voice that sounds like Amicus croaking. He slaps the arm of his wheelchair. "Old age is hard on Mr. Bell. And there isn't even much of that left. I say we stay outside. And please call me Jerry."

"How about the beach, Jerry?" Cooper's mother says.

Mary Ann frowns. "I don't know about—"

"The beach is fine," Mr. Bell says in his gravel voice.

The wheelchair is hard to push in the sand. Caddie helps. His mother helps. Cooper picks up sticks and rocks in the path. Together they push and pull and roll Mr. Bell's wheelchair across the mossy grass and down the hill to the beach and park Mr. Bell under the yellow leaves of the birch tree.

Cooper faces the hill. He wants Mr. Bell to be happy, but he can't see the road from the beach. What if Mike comes? What if Mike comes and doesn't know the party is on the beach?

"What's that?" Caddie says. She is pointing at the lake. Pointing at a boat. At two people in a boat towing something big and orange and otherworldly toward the dock. The contraption bobs and tips behind the boat. Its mast sways.

"Who is that?" Cooper's mother asks.

"Looks like Ron Tisdale. Richard's boy," Mr. Bell says. "And his son, Mike."

"Oh, Cooper," Caddie says, her cheeks turning pinker and pinker by the second. "Please tell me you didn't."

"What a coincidence," Cooper says.

They stand in a line. A line of strangers: Caddie, his mother, Mr. Bell, Mary Ann, and Cooper. And watch. Now Cooper knows what it felt like when Earthlings landed on Tezorene. The Tezornauts were looking forward, shaking with fear and excitement. And hope.

"What have you got there?" Mr. Bell tries to shout, but Mike cannot hear his crackle voice. The motor hums. The water slaps the hull of the fancy boat. The orange tanks echo.

"I reckon it's a raft," Cooper says.

"I was beginning to wonder where we would sit," his mother says. She puts her hand on Caddie's shoulder. Caddie tightens her lips. Frowns at Cooper.

"Ahoy!" Mike shouts, jumping to the dock. Mike

ropes the raft to a stanchion. Pushes the anchor over the edge and into the water. Ron cuts the motor.

"Ahoy!" Cooper shouts back.

"Is that you, Jerry?" Ron calls as he walks up the dock.

"Hell's bells, Ron. Who else do you know who's as old as the glaciers that made these ice-cold lakes?"

"How are you? I hear you've been sick."

"Still upright," Mr. Bell says.

Mary Ann covers her mouth. Ron laughs. Takes Mr. Bell's hand in both of his. Nods at Cooper's mother. "I hear you're having a party."

"It's all Cooper's idea," she says.

"You are welcome to join us," Cooper says. "But why are you towing the raft?"

"I was going to take it to the dump when Mike insisted we bring it here. That is, if you want it."

"We want it," Caddie says. "There's nothing to do up here."

"I put a mast on it for you, Cooper. We could take it out right now, if you want," Mike says.

Cooper freezes. Shivers in the hot sun. He does not want to take the raft out right now. Does not want to take the raft out ever. He backs up. Right into Mr. Bell's bony knees.

"We could have the party on the raft," his mother says.

Cooper holds his breath. Feels the Earth turn without him. He does not want to have the party on the raft.

"It's certainly big enough for all of us," Ron says.

"I don't think it's safe with the wheelchair and all," Mary Ann says.

Cooper exhales. Feels his shivers ebb like an ocean tide.

"I don't need my wheelchair," says Mr. Bell. "Unless you want to roll me off. Not a bad way to go, if you ask me." Mr. Bell laughs at his own joke.

"Jerry," Ron says, "you haven't changed a bit."

Mike walks down the dock. Looks into the motorboat. "I think we have enough life jackets."

Cooper stares at Mr. Bell. Can't believe he would make a joke about dying. *Can* believe he would do it all over again if he had the chance. Mr. Bell stares back at Cooper. Like a laser light show, Mr. Bell's stare pierces his eyes, his heart, his brain. Cooper knows. Cooper knows Mr. Bell knows that he is afraid.

"I'm game if you are, my boy," Mr. Bell says.

My boy.

Mr. Bell tugs on Cooper's hand. Pulls him close, so close Cooper can smell Swiss cheese, the smell of old age. Mr. Bell whispers in his clogged-drain voice, "If I can do it, you can do it."

Logic, preparation, and caution. Logic, preparation, and caution. Logic, preparation, and caution.

Mike tosses Cooper a life jacket. Cooper catches it. Drops it to the ground like a hot potato. A sand spider scurries under a twig.

Mary Ann puts on her life jacket. Helps Mr. Bell with his. Ron, Mike, Caddie, and his mother put on their life jackets.

Cooper does not.

He stands there with the life jacket at his feet. A life jacket is a misnomer. It does not give life. It gives hope. People he loves are going to get on the raft. The raft could sink. The raft could capsize. Hope is not good enough on a raft. He looks to the horizon. Storms can come out of nowhere. *Don't think. Don't think. Don't think.* Cooper shakes from the inside out.

"Hurry up, Coop," Caddie says. She picks up his life jacket. Holds it open. Like a robot, Cooper slips his arms through the holes. Caddie whispers, "It'll be okay."

If Cooper can go on the raft, then Mr. Bell can go on the raft. If, then. It is an equation. No, it is a theorem. Which means the reverse is true. There is logic in theorems. But he believes Caddie more than he believes this mathematical statement. "Are you sure?"

Caddie nods.

"Just a minute," Cooper says. "I need to prepare."

"Caddie," his mother says, "help me get the ice cream."

Cooper clips the life jacket's strap at his waist. "I'll be right back," he says.

"Don't forget the Jolly Roger," Mike yells.

Cooper runs ahead of Caddie and his mother. The screen door squeaks open and snaps shut. He runs to his room. Opens the fluffy plastic package from Ron's Bait Shop. Puts the giant fishing vest over his life jacket. The pockets hang at his knees, big and empty. They will hold his prized possessions: his rocks—the big one with the fossil; the one the size of his fist; the two smaller ones, like cardinal eggs; and the flat one, like a nickel—his magnifying glass, his notebooks and pencils, and Mike's book, *The Adventures of Tom Sawyer.*

He fills his pockets one prized possession at a

time. The rocks go in the big pockets at his knees. The notebooks go in the secret pocket near his heart. Mike's book goes in his breast pocket.

"Cooper, are you coming?" Caddie shouts.

"I am preparing," he yells.

The screen door squeaks open, snaps shut.

Cooper drops to his knees in his room. The rocks clunk against the wood floor. He reaches under his bed for the Jolly Roger flag. The flag of death. *Don't think about death. Don't think about death. Don't think about death.*

A pirate flag. The Jolly Roger. A gift from his friend, Mike.

Jolly, jolly, jolly. Jolly, jolly, jolly.

Amicus croaks. Cooper can't believe he almost forgot him. "Of course, you're coming too," he says. "It's a goodbye party for everyone." He scoops Amicus into the microwave-safe dish. Puts the strainer on top. Carries the Jolly Roger flag between his teeth.

His hands are full. He cannot run or he will spill Amicus. The heavy pockets knock at his knees with every careful step. Mike looks at him the way he did when he wore his Tezornaut helmet, but Mike holds his lips tight. Does not say, "Why are you wearing that?" Cooper tips his head and lets Mike take the pirate flag from his teeth.

"Argh," Mike says and hops up on the dock.

"But we're good pirates, Mike. We're the ice-cream-eating pirates."

"Aye-aye," Mike says as he steps onto the raft.

Mr. Bell gives Cooper a good long look. Cooper knows he looks ridiculous in a giant fishing vest. His hands are full or he would write this down:

Sometimes looking ridiculous is equal to logic, preparation, and caution.

"Hell's bells," Mr. Bell says. "What have you got there?"

Amicus looks ridiculous, too, in a bowl with a strainer on top.

"This is Amicus the Great. *Amicus* means 'friend' in Latin. He's brave, and he likes parties."

Mr. Bell holds out his hands for a closer look. Cooper gives him the bowl. And the strainer. The water in the microwave-safe dish ripples with little waves in Mr. Bell's shaking hands. "Well, Amicus," Mr. Bell says, "any friend of Cooper's is a friend of mine."

Caddie steps onto the raft. Sets the bowls and spoons and napkins next to the mast. His mother gets on the raft and sets down two big metal bowls of ice cream. They are covered with dish towels to keep out the bugs.

Standing next to Mr. Bell, waiting on the beach, Cooper shivers.

"Are you cold?" his mother calls to him.

Cooper shakes his head. He is not cold. He is hot. Boiling hot. And he has realized something very important. He is shivering with electrical impulses. He is dangerously riddled with electricity. Electricity so powerful he could ignite dead branches. He cannot step in the water. Cannot get wet. Cannot close the circuit or Mr. Bell's oxygen tank will explode. The raft will fly sky high. And everyone on it will sizzle and die. Cooper shivers so hard he cannot walk. Cannot lift one leg toward the dock. Toward the raft.

Caddie jumps off the raft. Wades to the shore. "Hurry up, Cooper." She takes Amicus from Mr. Bell. Places the frog's dish on the raft next to the bowls and spoons.

"Cover him up," Cooper says.

Caddie sets the strainer on top of the frog's dish.

Cooper scans the rippling silver lake. The lake is so big he cannot see across it. So small it is a dot in the universe. The raft is a microdot. Cooper is invisible. No one can see his fear. He imagines himself an illusion. An invisible illusion. An erroneous perception of nothingness.

Sometimes nothing is everything.

"Just a minute," he says. His hands are free. He can write that down.

"C'mon, Coop," Mike calls from the raft. "You're my first mate."

Cooper cannot disappoint Mike. He puts his notebook away. Steadies himself. He lifts one leg. Then the other. He walks like a shaky old man. Like Mr. Bell. And then he hears Mr. Bell's voice.

Logic. Another step toward the dock.

Preparation. One step closer to the raft.

Caution. One misstep away from total disaster.

Cooper stops.

Mary Ann hooks Betsy on the back of Mr. Bell's wheelchair. Takes off Mr. Bell's shoes and socks. Rolls his pants up to his ankles. His old feet are bumpy and blue and as dry as toast.

Mike grabs the oxygen tank. Mary Ann and Ron carry Mr. Bell. They set him down on the edge of the raft like a valuable statue. His blue feet disappear beneath the water.

The Jolly Roger flaps in the gentle wind.

I can do this. I can do this. I can do this. Cooper lifts one heavy leg. Then the other. *I must do this. I must do this. I must do this.* And if I do? *What if it sinks? What if it sinks? What if it sinks?* "How much weight does this rig hold?"

"A lot," Mike says.

"Can it sink?"

"Only with dynamite," Mike says. "Are you carrying explosives?"

Logic. This question is a question of logic. "No," Cooper says. The question is also a joke. But Cooper cannot laugh. Cannot throw caution to the wind. He *is* the explosive. "That's funny, Mike," he says. But it isn't funny at all.

Cooper has arrived at the edge of the raft.

"Give me your hand," Mike says.

Cooper extends his hand. Closes his eyes. But only for a second.

With one strong yank, Cooper is on board the otherworldly seagoing vessel. The raft bobs. The mast tips. Cooper gets down on his knees and crawls behind Mr. Bell. He keeps one arm around the mast, hanging on for dear life. Caddie jumps on board. Mary Ann gets on. His mother gets on. The raft heaves and rocks. Ron lifts the anchor, lands it on the deck with a thud. He coils the rope. Water drips and pools.

Mike unhooks the ropes. Shoves off from the dock with one foot. One bare pirate foot.

"Just a minute," Cooper says. Everyone looks at him. "I forgot to give you your book, Mike." He pulls *The Adventures of Tom Sawyer* from his breast pocket. "I finished it."

Mike takes the book. "Did you like it?"

Cooper nods. "I reckon it changed my life."

"Thanks," Mike says. Mike winds up, throws the book across the raft, across the water and across the sand. The pages barely flutter. The book lands in Mr. Bell's wheelchair. Right next to Betsy.

"You forgot Betsy, Mr. Bell," Cooper says.

Mr. Bell crackles with a laugh. "You know what that means." He taps his temple with a long, bony finger.

"This will be one of your best pictures ever," Cooper says. "Your magnum opus."

Mr. Bell laughs. And coughs.

Cooper closes his eyes. He is on top of a raft on top of water. Full of electricity. His whole body shakes like an outboard motor. He wants to touch. Wants to wash. Wants to count. Cannot count anything but seconds. *One, two, three . . .*

Voices hum around him like insects.

The oxygen tank hisses.

"Ellen," Mr. Bell says and then he coughs. "It was a day just like this one when your dad caught the biggest walleye on record in this county." Mr. Bell coughs again.

Thirteen, fourteen, fifteen . . .

"I remember," Cooper's mother says. "We got our picture in the paper. I was just a little girl, but he always took me fishing with him. He liked to say I had more patience than a lure."

Ron laughs.

"I took that picture," Mr. Bell says.

"Wow," Caddie says.

"My dad used to talk about that fish all the time," Ron says. "Back when he opened the bait shop. I think that was the beginning of the annual fishing contest."

"I didn't even know you liked to fish, Mom," Caddie says.

"I love to fish," she says.

"I know all the best places," Mike says.

"Maybe next year," she says.

Cooper shoves his hands in his pockets. Grips the rocks with all his might. *Forty-four, forty-five, forty-six . . .*

"Who's ready for ice cream?" Caddie asks. "We better eat it before it melts."

Ice cream. Cooper stops counting. Opens his eyes. The raft is not sinking.

"I'm always ready for ice cream," Mr. Bell says.

"Chocolate or strawberry?" Cooper's mother says.

"Both," says Mr. Bell.

Mike pushes them toward the lily pads with one long oar. "How deep is it here?" Cooper asks.

"Your waist or so. Look. You can still see the bottom."

Cooper inches to the edge. Peers at the brown and rippled sand beneath thin, green water. He spots a school of minnows. They do not swim in a circle like the minnows in Ron's Bait Shop, trapped and frantic. "Look at the happy cynprinnadae," he says.

"Cynprinnadae?" Mr. Bell says. "You sound just like your grandfather."

Mike puts the oar in the water again. Pushes them deeper.

"Here's your ice cream, Cooper," his mother says.

"Ice cream," Cooper says. He sits up fast.

"Cooper, watch out!" Caddie yells.

But it's too late.

Cooper's foot kicks the microwave-safe dish. Sends it into the air. Like a bubble. Sailing. The strainer left behind. "Nooo!" Cooper hears himself shout. The word arcs through the sky, a contrail of long O's.

Brave Amicus pokes his head into the air.

Cooper must save him.

He leaps from the raft. Flings himself into the wind. Into the water. Feels himself defying death to save Amicus. Feels the smooth plastic bowl slip through his fingers. *Almost. Almost. Almost.*

The dish falls away.

Amicus plunges.

Cooper holds his breath. Ducks below the surface. The water stings his open eyes. He sinks to the bottom. Cannot move forward. The rocks. The rocks are too heavy. They hold him back. He pulls the biggest rock from his pocket. The grandfather rock. Pulls out the others too. Drops them to the bottom of the lake. Feels himself freed. He rises. Reaches for Amicus. Reaches and reaches.

But Amicus swims with all his might. His long legs pump together. Perfectly. Automatically. Easily. Without a care in the world.

Cooper lunges. Feels the sand give beneath him like soft ice cream. He reaches. Reaches again.

Reaches one last time.

Amicus lifts his head toward the pink sunlight. Glows in the sunbeam for a second. Like a firefly. Disappears into the lily pads.

Amicus the Great.

Home where he belongs.

Cooper surfaces like a breaching whale. He spits water with a gasping breath. Rubs his eyes. The water laps at his chest.

"Did you catch him?" Caddie asks, leaning over the edge of the raft, her eyes as bright as the lilies.

Cooper shakes his head. "You should have seen him swim. He wasn't scared at all. I didn't know he could do that." Cooper catches his breath. "It was like he knew where he belonged the whole time."

The oxygen tank hisses.

Hisses with breath.

Hisses with life.

Cooper's hands and face drip with water. And then he remembers.

He looks at Caddie and Mike and his mother and Ron and Mary Ann and Mr. Bell. He can't believe his eyes. The raft did not blow up. His charged ions did not electrocute them. Did not incinerate the raft. Everyone is alive and well. They smile. They do not know they were in danger. Cooper shivers with disbelief.

"Your ice cream's melting," Mr. Bell says. "You better hurry before I eat it."

Caddie holds out her hand. Cooper grabs it. Climbs aboard the raft. Water drains from his giant vest, pools at his feet. He stops shivering. Feels the warmth of the sun. The warmth of a hundred years. The warmth of hearts still beating.

Sometimes you don't know you have done something brave until it is behind you.

He can write this down, right now. He unzips his vest. Reaches inside the secret pocket. Finds the notebooks, but they are soft and wet. All of them. He wants to stomp. Wants to touch and count and run, but he is trapped on the raft. He shoves his desperate hands into his deepest pockets. They are empty. The rocks are gone. Of course, they are gone.

Except, wait a minute. One rock is left behind. Stuck in the corner. One tiny, flat rock the size of a nickel. A souvenir of Amicus the Great.

Cooper turns the small, flat rock over and over and examines it like a specimen. There is only one place in the whole world the Amicus rock belongs. He looks to the shore, to Mr. Bell's wheelchair. To Betsy. Looks back at the rock. Knows he cannot write this down:

Sometimes you have to let go.
And then you can use both hands to hang on for dear life.

For a moment, Cooper watches Caddie and his mother. Mike and Ron. Mary Ann and Mr. Bell. Everyone is eating ice cream.

With the flat rock in his fingers, like a tiny discus, Cooper eyes the water. He holds his arm out straight, winds up, and sends the rock across the smooth and silvery lake toward the lily pads.

The rock sails just above the lake's surface. Touches down. Makes a tiny splash.

In a millisecond, the rock arcs through the air again. Lifting off like a small bird. Soundlessly. Hopefully. The rock bounces on the top of the lake one more time.

And skips through the air.

Into the pink sunlight.

AUTHOR'S NOTE

I was only three when my oldest sister, Catherine, boarded a plane to Germany as an exchange student, the year before she went off to college. So even in my earliest memories, she was always a grownup, a writer who liked to travel, a big sister who brought me jewelry, weavings and seashells from such faraway lands as Lebanon, Israel, and Honduras. But because we were so far apart in age, I knew almost nothing about my amazing big sister's childhood. Not until we were both grownups, and I had also become a writer, did I learn about what she had endured as a little girl.

At a literary event, I was in the audience as she read a short memoir. I had heard her read in public before, usually about her exotic travels, but this piece was different. This piece was about how, when she was ten years old, sudden fears took over her life. And then, for reasons she never understood, she withdrew into her own world and created rituals to protect everyone she loved from unknown harm. For more than two years, she did everything in threes, including reading. Just like Cooper, she read every word three times, every line three times and every page three times to keep her family from bursting into flames.

When Catherine read about our father's concern that, because of her strange behavior, she might hurt her new baby sister, I started to cry. I realized I was that new baby sister. And, as a mother, I was saddened that no one understood this lonely, frightened little girl. Not even our parents. Catherine's behavior scared *them*, but her account of her fears and her struggle broke my heart. It was then I decided to write a story that would honor both her inner turmoil and her bravery.

My sister suffered from what the medical world calls Obsessive Compulsive Disorder, or OCD. Some children are able to work through the condition. Some are helped by medications and therapy. For others, we hold out hope and ask that the world be patient, kind and accepting.

Catherine overcame the odds on her own. She graduated from high school and college with honors, learned several foreign languages, traveled the world alone and became a nationally recognized, award-winning travel journalist and photographer, as well as a beloved teacher, sister, wife, aunt, my mentor and friend.

After Catherine read *The Notations of Cooper Cameron* she sent me this note: "The book made me feel it again—the exhausting constancy of the isolation, that imperative of having to do more counting, more touching, more anything. You created a pitch-perfect portrait of how that old fear felt. I felt like Cooper—looking up from the edge of the water at the cabin, but finally being understood. Comforted. Rescued. How amazing to have healing drop out of the sky—and from my baby sister."

More than anything, *The Notations of Cooper Cameron*, like Catherine's, is a story of hope.

ABOUT THE AUTHOR

Jane O'Reilly is the author of the acclaimed middle grade novel, *The Secret of Goldenrod*, and the recipient of a McKnight Fellowship in Screenwriting. She also holds an MFA in Writing for Children and Young Adults from Hamline University. The youngest of five children, she spent her early summers traveling the country on family vacations and her teenage summers with her family in the North Woods of Minnesota at the cabin her grandfather built on Round Lake. Her children and grandchildren live out of state, but she and her husband live in their hometown of Minneapolis.